About the Author

D. Martines currently resides on the central coast of California. *The Rabbit Killer* is his first published story.

The Rabbit Killer

D. Martines

The Rabbit Killer

Vanguard Press

A CIP catalogue record for this title is
available from the British Library.

ISBN 978 1 80016 822 0

This is a work of fiction. Names, characters, businesses, places, events
and incidents are either the product of the author's imagination or used in
a fictitious manner. Any resemblance to actual persons, living or dead, or
actual events is purely coincidental.

*Vanguard Press is an imprint of
Pegasus Elliot Mackenzie Publishers Ltd.*
www.pegasuspublishers.com

First Published in 2024

**Vanguard Press
Sheraton House Castle Park
Cambridge England**

Printed & Bound in Great Britain

For Cynthia

New Places

The old rabbit burst through the tall grass, sprinted across a small open area, and then vanished into the nearest cover of old growth sage. It was a sudden and close chase. But now, it was hidden. Tucked beneath the shaggy and ancient chapparal, it lay as low as possible, its ears tucked tight against its body and its little head pressed against the earth. It was no longer a rabbit, but had become a lost shadow. For the time being, it was deep in a thicket, embraced in its cover, and out of play.

The brush snapped, popped and parted at the overgrown trailhead, as a young lioness slowly emerged and stepped into the clearing that her prey had crossed, just moments before. She stopped to listen, put her nose to the ground, could smell frightened rabbit, and then lifted her head for a deep whiff of this newly discovered area. She had never been to this place before, but she had passed the hidden trailhead to this place many times. Although the prey that had led her to this spot had escaped, it did not frustrate or concern her. Knowing that the rabbit had entered the brush line had caused her to immediately lose interest in some lucky rabbit. She was not that hungry at the moment, anyway.

Her ears constantly twitched and rotated at every chirp, click or twisting noise coming into the clearing from the busy forest. Her breaths were quick, and through her nose, as her olfactory senses processed the recent history of this fresh place. The big lion carefully slinked around the clearing, walking its small perimeter at a slow, casual pace. Small puffs of dust billowed out from beneath her wide and heavy paws, with each relaxed and brash step that she took. She calmly and indecisively inspected this latest prospect, purely for the sake of curiosity and lion comforts. So far, her inspection had revealed nothing intriguing, or necessary, in this new but typical clearing.

The cougar was on her last perimeter check, and just about to leave, when she saw it. She had walked right up to it, and there it was. She had rambled by it several times, but she just now noticed it. She stretched out her strong and sinuous neck, slowly leaned forward, and let her nose guide her towards the open mouth of an ancient granite cave, whose entrance was loosely covered by tall, dry grass and a tall ceanothus bush that was leaning over and trying to hide the entrance.

But the sharp-eyed cat could see beyond the old boughs, and into the almost hidden, deep hollow. And she knew that there was room in there for her. She sniffed at the entrance, pushed her face past the sparse, grassy cover, and then curiously entered the prehistoric relic.

The hollow rock shelter was vacant, and forgotten. She found the open and high-ceilinged cavern mysterious, and inspected it for several minutes, sniffing the empty corners, and finding no evidence of any dangerous inhabitant or opponent. She crept towards the back of the ancient chamber and discovered a narrow granite passage that was barely wide enough to squeeze through, and that led out of the cave, as the ancient lava tube swept upwards, like a vent, and exited through the top of the mountain. She pulled herself up and through the thirty-foot passage, and soon crawled from its narrow and rocky exit into a small granite clearing, on very high, flinty ground. The vista gave her a commanding view of the valleys below and exposed her to further distances that she could see, but not really comprehend, or find immediately relevant, as a mountain lion. So, she sat and stared out at the endless panoramic vista, smelling the uninterestingly pure high mountain breeze, and seeing no game.

She walked about the small peak, looking over all its ledges, and losing interest in its baren offerings. The big tawny lion looked out across the valley one last time, then slipped into the rock hollow, and returned to the interior. It was comfortable here. She felt safe and relaxed, and ready to sleep for the day.

Moving towards the rear of the old grotto, she eventually settled down onto a very rare and unusual monolithic slab floor, to begin her pre-sleep ritual.

Sitting like a sphinx, on her stomach with paws facing forward, and haunches in position to pounce, but very relaxed, with her head up and eyes wanting to close, she faced the entrance of the cave, watching for intruders, while adjusting to her new den.

She lumbered over onto her side and began to stretch. She noticed how the flat and near level floor supported her very large and heavy cat body. So, she rolled onto her back and was comfortable. It was a pleasant, unusual sensation, but not easy to maintain, as the floor was flat and did not stop her from rolling in either direction. She tried to balance on her spine, but was too heavy, and each time she tried to balance, she would roll over onto her side, sometimes her left side, sometimes her right side. But because the flatness of the floor was so pleasurable to her, she continued to roll back and forth for several minutes, before finally curving her body into a U shape that allowed her to balance on the smooth floor, with her spine down and giant paws held to her chest. She began to purr loudly, causing a low rumble that echoed throughout her new lair. She soon rolled over onto her side and breathed in deep, while reaching her sprawling limbs out as far as possible, into a big stretch. She let her heavy head rest on the cool, flat floor, and fell into an eventual sleep.

The big cat occupied the cave during her daytime slumbers for several weeks. As her confidence in the shelter grew, she began to spend more and more time around it, and eventually she began to bring small surplus game back to it, to consume in one feeding. After these quick meals, she would lick the last blood from the smooth floor beneath her, not unlike a person licking a big dinner plate, and then doze off on the cool slab, until she felt the urge to hunt again.

Daily she frequented a very small spring nearby, so she didn't need to travel to the bottom of the valley for seasonal water. And in this new, immediate territory, prey was very plentiful. And for these reasons alone, she would stay as long as the local game presented itself to her; She would stay as long as she could simply walk away from her secret lair, and then into the forest, to easily hunt rabbits, deer and sometimes small pigs, and then return to the shelter, to safely sleep away the daylight hours.

Typically, she left the cave to begin her hunt in the fading glow of the setting sun. Tonight, was no different. She routinely crawled up the tube that delivered her to the top of the saddled ridge, and then looked down into her valley. Often, she would sit to listen and observe before her evening hunt. Not unlike a person opening their refrigerator to see what to cook for breakfast. She could, at her leisure, survey the distant deer herds, rabbits and any animal that entered the valley below her all-seeing lookout. Some days she would sit there for hours, just watching, as if she were taking inventory of her own personal larder.

She had been watching her domain before a hunt, when a sudden and shockingly bright light in the sky had caught her attention. She had no idea what the light was, where it came from, or where it was going. But it startled and offended her, and caused her to intuitively crawl back down into the vent. She didn't know what she was hiding from, or if it was even a threat. But she hid from it, regardless.

Just as she had wound down the vent and emerged into her gallery, she heard footsteps, the rush and crunching of parting brush, and then, the most frightening sound of, "Here, bear!" echoed into the cave and reverberated throughout her lair. She did not understand why it was so loud and strange, or what it meant. Then it sounded again, "Here, bear! Bear! Bear!" getting nearer. Her adrenaline was peaking, and she was on the highest alert, feeling cornered, and ready to fight. The noisy intruder stepped into the small clearing, and then began walking towards the mouth of the cave.

It was not prey. It was not a bear, or another cat. It was the other type of animal that stood on two feet and behaved so mysteriously. The animal at the entrance may not be killed, but only feared. The lioness did not understand why the intruder was so dangerous, but she knew the danger was real, and deadly. The big cat began a low growl. She began to back up, giving herself room to receive whatever attack or challenge was surely coming. She turned about nervously and then, as if recalling something she had forgotten, quickly turned towards the back of the cave, and moved up the narrow vent space that exited above the ancient lost grotto. She suddenly emerged from the fissure, rushed low from its small peak, slipped over the ledge, and then slid down the steep granite sides and into the nearest heavy chaparral, easily disappearing into the forest, and escaping the invader.

The unwitting victor stood in the clearing, near the mouth of the cave, looking up into the sky, watching, just as the lion had watched, the final stages of a rocket's flight. She didn't know that a lion had been living in the cave. She wasn't aware of its presence or movements. She was, at the moment, mostly distracted by the technological display above.

Her arm moved towards her hood. She pulled it down and let out sweaty, brownish curls that fell about her shoulders. The road to this place was difficult, dangerous and relentless. This moment was the first moment, in many days, that she could consider a 'safe' moment.

She quietly stood in the clearing, watching a tiny, bright blue dot climb out of the atmosphere and vanish into outer space. Then, she just pushed aside the buckbrush, walked into the lion's den, and took over without contest. She was the supreme animal that had knowledge and control of all things. She could destroy all or save all. And she would live wherever she decided to live.

The bold intruder had been on the run for many days, and although relieved to have finally arrived at this place, she was also very tired. She had finally escaped the collective insanity of the remainder of civilization. And it wasn't easy. Intuitively, she had returned to the forest for peace, safety and wisdom. And now, here in a safe place, she could begin to process the truth of the repressed but inescapable, and inevitable questions, that had no acceptable answers.

Cupid

The massive object silently tumbled through the vacuum of space. It had been on its current trajectory for millions of years, and was moving at a preposterous, astronomical speed. It had so much momentum and solid mass that no local planet could survive, or recover, from even a glancing impact from this particular opponent.

It was first detected as it emerged from the constellation Cygnus, but its true origins were timeless and could never be known, without knowing everything about the universe itself.

At first it was referred to as an asteroid. But soon it was discovered to be an M-type pure nickel-iron minor planetoid. It was actually much smaller than what most people know as a planet, but it was big enough that, although it was indeed an asteroid, it might also be classified as a minor planet. Its composition suggested that it was likely the core of a much bigger planet that had been destroyed in the distant past. Perhaps it was once the size of Earth, but during its decomposition, it had survived as a much smaller remnant of the toughest part of its former self.

The object that remained was a mere two-mile diameter, solid nickel-iron bullet.

The young astronomy buff who had originally detected it, logged his first detection at about five-thirty a.m., on Valentine's Day. By noon on the same day, all observatories of the world were either studying, or preparing to study, this new development.

The object's discoverer, an amateur astronomer and social media enthusiast, knew early of its composition, as he had an inside friend at an observatory, who had confirmed the radar observations. Indeed, it was a nickel asteroid heading our way.

On this day, doing his best to follow tradition and name discoveries in honor of the Greek and Roman Gods, he called it Cupid. He began to release his videos on his social network, and soon that was the name that the world would call it.

Science was not impressed with the popular name choice that was given to the great global killer. And those truly interested and responsible for tracking the threat knew its officially recorded name as 2037LINEAR. The people who were working on the problem, and making constant reference to it, typically called it 'the object', while the president of the United States said it was 'our opponent', A clear and decisive call to arms against an un-tested and theoretical foe was initiated.

The responding world agencies and governments didn't really care about names and trademarks, or ten minutes of fame. They weren't really paying attention to social media. Their leading astronomers were too busy making calculations, and trying in vain to rule out the potential consequences that were so suddenly and coldly placed before them. But they were stuck, and could not rule out an absolute impact with one of our solar system planets.

When its trajectory was first calculated, many people found it ironic, that with its newly assigned name, and also the fact that it currently appeared to be on a bullseye run with Venus, that it should be named after the goddess's son. Venus, sister planet to Earth, was Cupid's final destination.

The world wondered: how would the destruction of Venus affect the Earth? Could we lose our orbit and fall into the sun? Or, could we be cast out of our solar system, to be lost to the vastness of space, on a frozen ball of secrets, that hides an upper layer of crushed relics and lost providence?

The people of the world immediately began the discussion of: Venus is about to take a huge asteroid hit, and what is the world going to do about it? And science calmly replied that even if Venus did take a hit, it would stay in its ancient orbit. Earth would not be affected. And it assured the world, that even with the colossal hit she was about to receive, Venus would stay put, and her cosmic beating would not significantly affect the perfect harmony of our sacred solar system.

The world began to feel hopeful again. Many people were so relieved that they stopped thinking about it. Others felt a type of survivor's guilt about the romantic planet; they wanted to continue research and action to save Venus, regardless of the unlikely, but possible effects that her disturbed orbit may have on our home planet. And during their continued campaign of research to save Venus, science had discovered an error, a miscalculation that was made early on. In the heat of their earliest efforts, they had accepted this error, and sadly, had assumed that it was correct. But it was wrong.

Shockingly, the original distance that was accepted and entered into all computer models to formulate the calculus, was incorrect by about fifteen A.U., or roughly a billion miles, give or take a few million miles. And one fact was now certain: there was no way Venus would be hit.

A huge sense of relief fell over the few who knew this new fact. There was a festive sort of atmosphere in many small, privy astronomy circles, and they were glad that soon they would be releasing this good news to the world. But first, they found it prudent to keep the new data secret until they could properly run the computer models to track the asteroid's true path. This would not be another comical error made in a panicked haste. These new numbers would be run many times, and peer reviewed constantly for accuracy.

So, they fixed the numbers and recalculated the flyby. However, the new scenario revealed a grim new prediction. And as fate would have it — especially in Greek plays — an adversary stepped in to upset the balance, and threaten the plot. Soon it was known, to a sad and horrified world, that Cupid would not make it to Venus, but instead, Gaia would order Earth and her armies to place themselves in the path of Cupid, as an answer to Cupid's threats, and claims of cosmic hierarchy.

The public did not handle the news of the approaching asteroid well.

At the same time that the Certain Earth Impact Theory was announced, humanity had also been busy colonizing our nearest planet and moon. The rocket industry was thriving. But most of the world was not involved in space, or the business of space, and their societies broke down fast. Because, once people had accepted the certain fact that their planet was scheduled to be destroyed, there was no longer any desire, or reason, for them to serve any master, for any price, any more.

Most people simply resigned from their important roles and jobs to wait out the remaining time in peace, on their own terms, hoarding food, and establishing a defendable space. But they would soon find out that no matter what they did, peace would never find them, and that their abandonment of all things only served to make their remaining existence more tortuous.

Food and fuel sources were immediately raided. When resupply fell short, food shipments were hijacked. Starvation had begun. Power shut down and was lost to most of the planet, as loyal employees, far outnumbered by their fleeing counterparts, were unable to maintain plants, supply lines or security. The military was preoccupied with defending its own critical resources, trying to mitigate its own desertions, and with such limitations, it was unable to assist or defend any civilian effort to maintain order.

Resources were carefully escorted to places and persons who were still involved in, and still interested in, the last battle for humanity. And only those who felt a higher calling above their own comforts and fears remained to fight a lost battle. And although they were very few in number, they stood as the true warriors, willing to give all, in defense of the planet called Earth, home of the many souls who were the only witnesses and protectors of her existence.

A Secret Spot

Adela awoke to a storm.

Heavy showers had begun in the early hours, but by the light of dawn, as if on cue, the night's fitful storm had slowed to a light, gusty drizzle. The storm wasn't completely over; it was just on the move, making way for the next storm that was to follow.

The night had been cool, so she was deep down inside her sleeping bag, curled up and comfortably warm.

Thunder clouds were building off in the distance. As the brunt of the storm got closer, she could hear the rumbling thunder and the distant lightning strikes, and feel the high pressure of the approaching storm tingling throughout her body.

She curled up tighter and tried to move deeper into her bag. But even though she tried to hide from the lightning, the bag's material was not thick enough to block the arc light of the return stroke, and she could plainly see the white flash that suddenly illuminated stitching patterns and a hint of blue fabric, up close and mostly out of focus, with each lightning bolt flash. And then three seconds later, the shock wave from the massive electrostatic discharge would roll through the valley, and smash into the mountain range. She flinched at the sudden shock of the thunder that was followed by a low rumble, as it reverberated through the valley, and into the far corners of the granite cave that had been her home for several months.

She could stay warm and stay put, at least for a day or two, if that was what she wanted.

And on a day like today, it would be completely justified and well deserved to do nothing. After all, it was raining. She knew that she had food and water for days, and her shelter was dry and safe. However, she had rabbit traps out.

A person couldn't just not check their rabbit traps, regardless of the weather. You didn't just break your own rules about rabbit traps simply because you had a cozy warm bed. Besides, these traps were close by, and she only had two out, anyhow. She knew that they were likely sprung and waiting. And she also knew that if she left them out too long, another animal could find them.

She pushed her arms through the bag's collar while stretching her legs and pointing her toes into the foot of the bag. Arching her back, she roared like a little animal as the relief of the morning stretch prepared her for the morning rise. The reaching arms pulled back into the warm bag, as she slowly pulled down the bag's zipper around her face, and peeked out beyond the warm collar of the down filled, cocoon like refuge.

She could see that the inside of her shallow cave was still dark, but the slightest dawn wanting in. The rain was mild now, and the higher winds from the night before had calmed to light breezes, with the occasional, gentle gust. The storm runoff had formed rivulets and a little stream near the cave entrance. A small puddle had formed on the flat rock floor, inside, near the entrance, and it glinted at her. Adela looked towards the sparkle, and thought that she had never seen a puddle form there before.

She sat up and scratched her head, reached up towards the ceiling, and gave a long, vertical, and eventual standing stretch to celebrate an undisturbed patch of comfortable slumber. She reached for the ceiling as the bag fell around her feet and legs. She lowered herself back down onto her thick fabric nest, and sitting lotus style, leaned over and pushed her hands through her nearby small mound of clothes and belongings, letting her hands feel their way through the soft heap until she found her water bottle. She pulled it free from the small clothes pile and unscrewed the cap. She emptied the container in one greedy chug, and then stood up again.

There was a small window-like opening on her west wall that looked out across the nearby valley, and she went to it. She stood on her toes and peered out through the small roundish opening. She could see the clouds in the distance that were parting, as beams of light pierced through, rolling huge swaths of sunlight across the shaded, green grass valleys below. She stepped back and looked over at her cozy sleeping place, once again contemplating its luxury and protection from the elements.

The world was becoming more illuminated by the minute. She knew it was at least six thirty a.m. because she could now see the snake and the bear etched into the walls, near the back of the cave. As the morning crept in, it lit up the dark corners, and began to bounce its light around and throughout the space, and was sure to light up even the darkest corners of her rocky home.

She could not, in a million years, have imagined that she would ever be here again under any circumstances other than casual recreation. But here she was. Somehow, she had found her way back to this familiar and safe place, for reasons that could not have been predicted.

This was her late family's traditional and secret spot. It was everybody's favorite hike. They all looked forward to the frequent excursions to the remote camping, and the hidden caves of the Sierra Madre mountains. But this was a special place.

When she was two years old, she was carried to this shelter by athletic and energetic parents, who loved to camp here at least a few times each year. Her father was a professional archeologist and her mother was his field assistant. Naturally, they had considered these wild and remote places to be necessary retreats, to be returned to and inspected. And because of the nature of their work and their passion for wild places, they felt a responsibility and an accountability to the land. It was as if as if they had an obligation to know it and understand it, watching the land, watching its use, protecting its most fragile secrets, and enjoying its vastness and solitude. This was the steadfast position and attitude that Adela had adopted from her parents, from an early age.

Finding their way to this secret place meant three days of steady, not too strenuous hiking. But it was their favorite place, with exciting sites to explore, and surprise discoveries with every trip.

They could have moved faster if they didn't have a toddler with them, but they weren't going to let parenthood stop their passion for archeology, discovery and adventure. And they had neither the financial resources nor the desire to leave Adela behind with a babysitter. So, they simply brought her with them, and included her in their research and discovery efforts. It was that easy.

After a few years of being carried for at least part of the expedition trail hikes, she was eventually able to complete the entire route under her own power. By the age of seven, she no longer needed to be carried, most of the time. Of course, her parents paced the hikes and made sure that she stayed hydrated, and safe. But as time went by, her parents began to depend more and more on Adela as a solid and capable, back country hiking partner. And so, they explored much of the Sierra Madre mountain range in Central California together, as a family.

Everybody has a secret spot. Or at least they think they do. Adela and her parents had considered her now current home, as their 'secret spot'.

Her family never camped inside this cave, or used fire near it, when they came here to visit. They used to camp outside, in the suitable and level clearing right outside the entrance. Her father had too much respect for the site as an artifact, and he needed the space empty and free of any item that would impede his observations. He was always careful with fire pits and any other impact that their camping activities might have on the site. So, when he inspected it, he was careful where he stepped, and he certainly would not bring his family inside to sleep and roll around in this unique place. He would allow Adela to play inside if she was careful and respectful. And she made sure when, at times, she could not help herself from secretly touching the petroglyphs of bears and snakes and suns and lizards, that she touched them gently.

She loved this site as a child, and has always felt safe here. That's why she returned. It is the very place that she wants to be, if the world is truly ending. And although there is no hope for humanity, and even though civilization has so far been dismantled and replaced by random acts of anarchy, Adela sleeps here now. Inside. She sleeps a sound sleep, hidden from the worst monsters, and protected by her sacred menagerie of animals, sprit guides and ancient symbols that are etched on the walls and ceiling of her secret spot.

There is a little spring nearby, near the ridge top, and it flows at a slow steady rate, year-round. The water is good and drinkable, but Adela always boils it anyway. Her father showed her the spring when they first camped here. He guided her along a path near the cave that led to a gurgling little pocket of cool water, that flowed into a little pool, spilled over into a rock pile, and then drained not into a creek, but back into the rocky crags and crevices that seeped back into the earth, without leaving any indication of its wet salvation to any who would scan the horizon looking for such things.

She is hopeful that others won't come here. She hopes that they are too afraid to come out so far. She hopes that this place is simply not an option in their panic-stricken minds.

These memories flowed through her mind as she watched the forest through her little rock window. She turned away from the rocky aperture, and began to busy herself by immediately packing and stowing her gear. She likes to have everything ready to go, before finding breakfast.

She folds her extra clothes and refolds a few items before pushing them into her pack. She grabs her water bottles and fastens them to her pack. She then picks up her little gas stove, pauses, thinks about packing it, and then sets it down. "Kind of useless without fuel," she says out loud. She looks around and sees that the cave is clean and dry, her rabbit pelts put aside, and her acorn cache is in order.

Adela slips her arms through the shoulder straps of her pack, rocks back from her knees, and stands with her pack on. She does a small hop to settle her load, then cinches up the hip belt. Pulling her rain poncho over her head, she turns and walks toward the cave mouth. The rain is beginning to lighten up.

She had hoped it would keep raining hard. She feels a certain security in a hard rain, especially when she is out in it. She pulls her hood over her head, and cautiously emerges from her cave.

Meat Hunters

Stepping from rock to tree root, she avoids stepping in soft places, or in places where a footprint could betray her. She moves down the sensitive paths, doing her best to leave no sign, evidence or indications that could, and most likely would, lead others to her.

Eventually she comes to a fire road and pauses at the brush line. She slows her breath and listens. She hears birds singing in the lightest rain, and water dripping from the trees. A gust of wind shook droplets from the tall oaks all at once, causing them to come crashing down as a heavy spray. She thought it sounded like someone had thrown a handful of gravel into the brush. She listened a bit more, and then crept up the red rock shoulder to have a better look.

The road was clear. It was old and rarely used, even in the days before. The Forest Service did not maintain roads that weren't critical to their operations. This road was not essential, so it was allowed to fall apart, and its condition only got worse, day by day, especially during the winter. She doubted anyone would attempt to drive this eroded and forgotten old skid. It wasn't passable for most, and it didn't really lead anywhere, anyway.

She stepped out onto the road, looked right, then turned left and slowly walked along the shoulder. Occasionally she would pause to look carefully behind her, and her eyes constantly scanned the horizon. She often checked the road bed for footprints, hoofprints or tire marks. She had not seen any signs of people in this area since she had arrived, and that was understandable.

As long as people stayed connected to the remaining services of city infrastructures, she knew that she could be safe here. So, she made an extra effort to pull back and away, and hide herself far out in the center of what was previously known as public land.

Of course, there were no guarantees of any stable scenario in these final days. She knew that the effort of being remote is not enough; She must also hide, and avoid leaving any trace or indications of her activities or presence.

The one variable in her strategy that continuously threatens to defeat her survival plan is always the presence of animals, because animals might attract hunters. But she was so remote, and she hopefully doubted that there was really enough time to chase the balance of the edible mammal supply this far back into the wilderness.

She had seen hunting parties while on an excursion far away from here, nearer the coast. But luckily, they didn't see her. She remembered that they looked shabby and un-organized, unprofessional, and dangerous. She knew this was a new class of nimrod. She called them meat hunters when she talked to herself.

Meat hunters are people who scour the cities, hillsides and forests for game. There is nothing sporting about their methods, there is only the hunt, driven by hunger, and the power that comes with the controlling of the food that drives their hypothetic economy. Meat is power; currency in a world about to disappear.

You might be surprised at how fast an unstocked grocery store can be stripped of all its goods. Or how fast a crop can fail without a farmer tending to it. In these times there were no more crops. Only living meat, and whatever preserved and canned rations remain, since the news.

Adela remembered the final days, of her struggle to stay within the perceived safety of her once loved city.

After the news had alerted the world, all the grocery stores in her town were predictably looted, and all the food desperately captured by the next morning. There were no police to stop them. Many of the looters *were* police officers who had abandoned their posts and oaths, and had joined in the panicked, roiling mass of humanity.

People were looting food, and then trying to escape, get away from others to protect their precious stocks of hoarded food. But there was nowhere to run, and no solution to the problem. The world was swept up into a futile panic, and the crisis of humanity was no longer over-population and pollution, but the abandonment of all things.

Then there was no food. So, meat hunters formed desperate groups to scour the forests for game, Mainly deer, cattle, pigs and horses.

Many weeks earlier, Adela had a very close encounter with a band of meat hunters while exploring and gathering, about twenty miles from her beloved spring.

She was crossing a valley floor, and reluctantly walking a small section of open road, when she heard the slightest din of what sounded like voices. She stopped, held her breath, and listened. She could hear the careless and loud advance. As the gang approached a bend in the road, their voices grew louder.

Her adrenaline peaked and she desperately wanted to run the road, away from the approaching menace. But that would be the wrong move and she knew it, so she fought the desire and looked for a hole, an escape in the immediate vicinity. But there really was nowhere for her to go, but over the road shoulder, and into a shadowed jumble of large, loose boulders that had been strategically dumped as a retaining element for an old diversion channel, that had likely raged, and drained the small valley during winter storms.

She willingly leapt over the road shoulder, slid down the loose gravel bed, got turned head first as the weight of her pack's inertia pulled her off balance, and she rolled toward the field of big rocks. When she came to sudden stop, she found herself lodged in between two large boulders of granite. She wasn't hurt from the fall, but she was certainly stuck. There was no way she could have run away at this point, but that wasn't important. Most importantly, she knew, was that she was out of sight and hidden. And if they had heard her, or seen her, or if they had even cared about any sign that she may have left, as she went over the road shoulder, then she could have been discovered. But they didn't care about, or understand these types of details, so they didn't notice her. She had become invisible and could remain as such, so long as she could stay still, be silent and breathe slow, and even breathless, as she waited for them to pass.

About eight armed men walked on by, arguing loudly about a girl at their camp, completely distracted from their mission, and unconcerned about the volume of their stupidly loud voices.

She listened to their idiotic banter as they carelessly stumbled past. She thought they sounded vulgar and mean, and she thought that if they were looking for game, they sure weren't going to find it with those loud mouths.

After the gang had passed, she slowly released the clips of her harness, easily squirmed out of her pack, and was instantly free of the granite trap. She cautiously crawled out of the rip rap, and then crept up to the road shoulder to have a look, first checking to make sure that there weren't any stragglers following up the rear, and then slowly stretching out her neck just enough to see the backs of eight dirty hunters, walking down an abandoned road, on their way to find meat.

She doesn't like groups of people. Not now. Before the law was lost, sure, a group of people was normal. But now? No.

Her experience had taught her that a group of people in a time of lawless abandon can only be a dangerous gang. Her hatred for gangs, or even groups of people, was now personal. She knew that this gang wasn't any different than the first gang she had to deal with, and it reminded her of her first narrow escape, recalling to herself the brutality of the city gangs.

When she was still living in the city and hiding in the relative safety of her parents' home, she came to realize that these desperate groups of frightened and terrible people would soon arrive. After the news, mass shootings were common, rape was common, and home invasion became the norm. She knew that eventually a gang would hit her home, pillage its contents, and terrorize her, or worse. If they could catch her.

On the night that she had fled from her home in the ruined city, she had prepared herself well. She had on all of her darkest and warmest clothes and she was ready to run. She had been up for the last two days and nights, and she really needed sleep. But on this, her last night in her house, the sounds of violence in the distance were getting louder, more frequent and closer. She was too terrified to sleep, and too angry to run. So, there she stayed, on the floor, in the corner, looking up toward the big windows of her dark and powerless living room.

She no longer hoped for a miracle, or thought that maybe something would change, or that things would go back to normal, or that she could somehow stay. She knew that the cascading waves of anarchy were randomly striking house to house, with a very businesslike and efficient momentum. And although she did her best to maintain her place in the path of the inevitable destruction by mad men, in the face of impending doom, she knew that she must escape and never return.

This had been her home since she was in the first grade. Her parents had moved many times, but this home had been hers all through her adolescent and teenage years, and well into young adulthood. She loved this house and always felt safe inside its warm and functional design. This family home used to represent safety, security and family. It represented the things that no longer exist. Now, it is a completely obsolete and unsafe place to be. Any argument to the contrary, in her mind, would simply be denial. It was almost time to go; the moment was fast approaching.

There was no power, no gas, no phone service and no internet service. Her town was blacked out and in a state of total chaos. And so, she sat in the corner listening. The explosions in the distance and the crackling of small arms fire were moving in. She wanted to stay, but she knew that would soon be impossible.

There was no reason to stay anyway, she argued with herself. Her mother was never coming home. She knew that by now. Her mother's fate was her constant thought for these past weeks. It would have been easy enough for her mother to make it back by now. She went out after the announcement, and never returned.

Adela had to assume that she had snuck off to find food, because she wouldn't just run away with nowhere to go. No. That's not her. She wouldn't do that. However, she would sneak out to get food without telling Adela, so that Adela wouldn't be part of her dangerous food gathering mission. Now, that would be something that she would do. She's always trying to protect Adela. "See what happens? See what happens when you don't share your plan?"

Adela whispered to nobody. She knows she won't be back. She knows she is lost and will never come home again.

And all of her friends were certainly hiding, running, or swept into a gang or church. So really, there is no reason to stay any more, she decided.

"To stay is dangerous!" she heard herself say out loud. She felt a bit light headed at the realization of this fact. So, she sat on the floor, in the dark corner, and leaned back against the padded skirt of her favorite sofa. She let her head rest on its cushions while she looked up into the dark rafters and beams hiding in the shadows overhead. The woodwork was personal to her as she had helped her father install it not too many years ago. She could vividly recall the smell of fresh cut fir and pine, eating tuna fish sandwiches for lunch, and countless trips to the hardware store. "You did a really nice job on the knotty pine ceiling, Dad," she whispered quietly to the ghost of her late father.

She closed her eyes, and put her hands flat against her face to cradle her racing mind. As she pressed her fingers against her closed eyes, she could see little dots of light on the insides of her eyelids that appeared to vibrate and dance around. She thought they looked like they were trying to escape her vision, because every time she tried to focus on a tiny dot of light, it would move away, out of her periphery. She gently smiled and barely laughed to herself at the idea of it being a distracting little game.

She breathed in deeply, reluctant to leave the home that was, at one time, a place of urban security and peaceful enjoyment.

The fast-approaching sound of a roaring engine broke her meditation. Adrenalin coursed through her spine as it grew louder. The fear would not let her breathe. She sat terrified and motionless.

The large truck that roared into her driveway, finally got her to move. The headlights beamed through the living room window as it pulled off the concrete driveway, and onto the lawn. She winced as the high beams of the approaching invaders scanned through the big picture windows of her living room, temporarily blinding her, and causing her to quickly flatten out, onto her back, to avoid being seen, or cast a revealing shadow. She heard men jumping out of the truck and orders being shouted.

She rolled onto her stomach to stay as low as possible, then crawled along the floor to the hallway. When she reached the hall and was out of view of the big windows, she stood up, grabbed her pack, ran through the kitchen, and then out through the back door. The gang kicked in her front door just as she was climbing the back fence to jump into the neighbor's yard. She landed in Ute Larson's empty and abandoned garden, and then ran to her back gate that let out onto a dirt alley, used mainly for garbage pickup — when garbage pickup was still a thing — and then she sprinted through streets that were strangely silent, but for the roars of quick violence, and screams that were suddenly silenced, and never to be heard again.

She jogged through dark neighborhoods, hiding from any person or automobile that she saw; trying to be tactful, and keep her wits about her. She ran with her large pack bouncing, at a pace that she knew she could maintain for at least a few miles. It was her intention to run away, beyond the boundaries of civilization, away from the desperate necessities of humanity. Eventually she made it to the edge of her town, beyond the commercial areas and big box stores, and then into the foothills that gently sloped up through cattle ranges and large farm tracts. And then, finally, deep into the wilds of the Sierra Madre range.

Adela often thinks of those dangerous days, and she knows there is more uncertainty ahead. But on this particular day, she feels safe. So safe in fact, that if she didn't have traps out, she would take a day off.

While walking the old mountain road, she soon comes to a deer trail. She stops, looks behind her, then leaves the road, following the narrow trace down an embankment, and then across a small field leading to a tree line. Then, crouching over, she moves under a low branch, and then into a dark and damp oak forest, down a very wet and narrow, grass lined rabbit trail, that leads to her first trap.

A Rabbit's Tale

The young cottontail nosed through the dewy patch of clover. She was out early this morning, as usual, to feed on the freshest sprouts from the last rain. Her babies were back in the nest, snug and warm. They were used to their mother rising before dawn every morning, then leaving them behind as she went off to forage. The babies were not really 'babies' any more. They were almost two and a half weeks old by now. Almost old enough to move out and start families of their own. But they loved their nest, it was cozy and safe, and a fun place for rabbits to live.

It was tucked deep in the low growth shrub of the oak woodland, in the old burrow of a long gone badger. A large boulder over its entrance served as an impenetrable header that even the meanest predator couldn't move. Mama rabbit was born here, and she liked the area so much that she stayed, and had her babies here too.

To mama rabbit, this morning was just like any other blissful morning in the ample forest. The sparrows began to awaken, and welcome the morning with heartfelt songs of life and hope. A covey of quail began to stir in the undergrowth, with little scratching noises, and whispers of wails and calls yet to come. They began their little march from their night time cover, past the clover grazing mama rabbit, and towards the edge of the forest on their way to the seeds and favorite foraging sites in the low chaparral.

The little herbivores and small animals in this part of the densely overgrown and dark forest all tolerated each other very well. They knew who the real threats were, and they were always glad to see their other forests friends being calm, and browsing and grazing, like them. A person witnessing their interactions might even suggest they are polite to each other, yielding to each other, and watching out for each other. Mama rabbit practically said good morning to the covey that filed past her. As each little quail stepped past her, they let out a little peep. She stopped grazing for a moment, acknowledged the little regiment with a chew-less pause, then went back to her tender leaves. Such conversations were common in this community, and a big reason the current residents are so reluctant to relocate.

Rabbits in this type of cover, in such a lush setting, don't need to drink every day. They get their moisture from the plants that they eat. But they do love water, and will go to it if it's available to them. This morning, mama rabbit could smell the water from last night's rain. She knew there were big puddles out there, but they wouldn't last. She started to move down a well-worn trail, deep in her thicket, toward the lower ground, nearer the deer trails, where large pools had formed.

Normally she wouldn't bother to go this far, but a nice drink of water is something that was almost impossible for her to resist.

Finally, after negotiating the maze of rabbit trails, rabbit tunnels, rabbit underpasses and rabbit bridges, she reached the end of the thick undergrowth that grew through the lush oak forest. She sat up on her haunches, and twitched her whiskered nose as she peered out from her tunnel like trailhead, that terminated at the edge of the clearing. She could now see the large pools of water that had formed in the great meadow, the sweet smell was irresistible. She felt safe; it was only a few feet from cover, and she could easily run back into the thick brush at the slightest threat.

She tucked in her ears, dropped her front paws forward on the damp trail, brought up her big hind feet, then launched herself into a deliberate leap from the edge of the thick undergrowth, towards the open area, where she rarely goes.

And it was a fine hop, but something was different this time. Something about this casual leap was wrong. Something was stopping her. How strange, to hop forward, but not go forward. She would try it again, but with more force this time. Again, she jumped with more force, but instead of going forward, she violently lifted up, twirled in the air, then came crashing down with a thump.

She kicked and flailed, and spun and twisted, but nothing would free her. She even tried kicking her feet as fast as she could, causing little rocks and sticks to flip into the air and off into in the grass, but even that did nothing but exhaust her. Finally, she resolved herself to pulling away from the mysterious force that held her. Her rabbit mind reasoned that if you walked into it, you must back away from it. So, she pulled with all her might, while the wire noose tightened around her neck, threatening to suffocate her. Although it became tighter and tighter, she continued to pull and pull until she could no longer breathe. Her mouth was open but she could not cry out. Her eyes were wide open, but she could not see. Her life drained away while she gently rolled and twitched on the grassy trail. Her final rabbit thought was about escape, and how wonderful it would be to bound away through fields of deep clover.

Cooking pots

Every time Adela returns to her traps, she fully expects them to be sprung with cottontails in them. It almost never fails. So, as she was nearing the first trap, she was thinking of rabbit recipes.

She had been cooking them on skewers recently, and that worked very well. But you get tired of convenience food sometimes. She decided a nice rabbit stew would do.

Since coming here, she has discovered that a cooking pot is critical to living off the land. Ironic, but definitely true. If you're not smart enough to make your own cooking pot, you better bring one.

When she first arrived, she didn't have a cooking pot, in fact, she had nothing. Those days were extremely rough. All her food was roasted on skewers. Roasted food is tasty, but a pot of water is nice for preparing broths, soups, and stews. Tubers, berries, and other edible plants are often more palatable in a soup or stew. Also, when processing the acorns, multiple pots for boiling water make the job possible.

She had developed a taste for her leached and roasted acorns. They had a nice dry crunch that turned into a creamy butter texture when chewed, very much like peanut butter. She liked to roast them on the dark side. It gave them a nice smoky flavor, with the lightest aftertaste of tannin, about like a cup of tea.

Rabbits are extremely lean, so you must supplement your diet with fats from other sources, like birds, deer or acorns. If you make a nice rabbit stew, you can make the rabbit more nutritious, and tasty, especially with sage, bay leaves or many other aromatic herbs available in the forest.

She had been eating mainly roast rabbits, birds and a fawn that she managed to catch.

She didn't actually catch it, as much as stumble upon it.

She was walking through some tall grass and she found the little mule deer fawn hiding in the grass. He was curled up in a little nest, and trying to be as motionless as possible. And he did a great job too. But he couldn't hide from her. She had been eating a lot of rabbit and needed a diet change, so with very little hesitation, she scooped up the little baby, and made incredible jerky. She also saved the precious soft hide for tanning. If she had a pot back then, she could have made a hearty stock as well.

Luckily, one day, she found a pot and a small iron frying pan in an old campground. The two-quart pot was missing its lid, but it changed her life. Suddenly she could boil water, make stews, leach acorns and even bake. The frying pan allowed her to roast nuts or pan fry.

One day, not long after finding the first pot and pan, she found an abandoned vehicle under some very old pines. As she scavenged through the wrecked camper, she found two more pots.

It wasn't a new wreck that she had found, it had probably been wrecked and abandoned out here, in the middle of nowhere, many years ago. She wasn't a car expert, but guessed that the old RV that had been pushed under the trees, and covered in multiple layers of pine needles and branches, was about thirty or forty years old. She pulled a four-quart stock pot and a two-quart saucepan from that old pile of abandoned dreams. Strangely, there really wasn't much else left behind to rummage through.

Now she keeps two pots nested together and hidden away near a narrow but deep creek, where she does her acorn leaching, and one two-quart pot and frying pan at her main camp.

Anne

The weather had cleared and the rain more or less stopped. Adela was glad that she had decided to get out of the cave this morning. She was feeling strong, healthy, and in a strange way, content. She had become comfortable in these inevitable days, and appreciated the smallest of conveniences. She knew that her relatively stable situation was due to her hard work, and she took nothing for granted. Although she had much pride in her current state of security and plenty, she also knew that it could all be taken from her, and she could be pushed away from this place, if she was careless, or unlucky.

She reached into her pocket and pulled out a small handful of nuts. She popped them into her mouth and crunched them up one at a time, while she quietly followed the narrow and covered path. Today she'll pull up her trap line. She'll go somewhere else for rabbit for a while and give this area a break. Maybe try for other game, quail, or deer.

She typically likes to trap rabbits deep in the forested areas, but when she saw a well-used rabbit trace emerging near the road bed, she found the tunnel entrance to be a perfect place for the wire. She could tell this little insignificant trace was ancient. It had never had a trap near it, so it was impossible to not catch a rabbit there. It was too hard to resist. So, on her return to this trap, she wasn't surprised to find mama rabbit in the snare. She removed the wire noose from the delicate neck, turned it about to look for any defects, and then felt the weight of the catch. She smiled, and was satisfied that this one was young, and plump. Mama rabbit was a nice catch.

She collected the wire from the trap and put it in her pocket. She looked around and surveyed the area. Something felt wrong to her.

Yesterday, when she had placed the trap at this spot, she thought it was a good place to trap rabbits. But today, she's had a change of heart; she doesn't like how exposed it is. She'll be more careful in the future. She won't trap here any more.

She bound the rabbit's feet with a piece of para cord, and then tied it to her pack belt. She held the rabbit in her hands and stroked its soft face and ears, admiring its size and health. When she let it fall from her hands, it flopped against her thigh, upside down, with little ears hanging down, and little front paws that looked to be reaching for the ground. She continued on. The little cottontail gently bounced against her thigh with each step that she took, as she moved further down the path, into the dripping oak forest, and through a very dark and overgrown trail, barely wide enough for a small deer to get through.

She followed the path deep into its hidden and shadowed interior, and soon came to her second trap. She always had good hunting in this part of the forest, so she was not surprised to find a strangled cottontail in this trap as well.

He was plump, almost two pounds. She admired the mottled brown and white fur that was always very soft and luxurious on every rabbit that she had ever trapped. She thought rabbit fur was the softest thing that she had ever touched. She always found herself petting her dead rabbits.

She removed the noose from his little neck and turned him upside down, holding him by the feet. She took a piece of string and tied one end to his feet, and the other end to her pack belt, next to mama rabbit. The rabbits dangled upside down, and swung back and forth as she gathered up her wire and removed the trap from the trail. Finally, she put the wound-up wire into her pocket.

The rhythm of the forest was suddenly broken by an intrusive racket, from some type of commotion that was heading her way. Her adrenaline shot up, and she tried to stay calm while she desperately tried to understand the source of this frightening and sudden noise.

She stopped her harvest and stood perfectly still, holding her breath and listening. She heard the sound get louder as it passed along the road above, and echoed down into the forest. She could hear heavy breathing, gasping and stumbling with clumsy footsteps, coming from the gravel road above. It sounded like a person out of breath, in distress, worn out, but still moving as fast as they could. It was now obvious to her that this person was desperately running from something.

She crouched low in a squatting position, trying to stay hidden, but intrigued at the movement up on the road. Slowly, she began walking along the trail that led up to the road. As she got closer to the top of the trail, she paused, held her breath, and could hear more heavy, frantic breathing, with little whimpering fits.

She was close enough now to peer over the road shoulder. She crept up, then warily peered through the brush and tall grasses that grew from the steep shoulder of the road.

She could see a woman, about thirty, wearing torn slacks, a dirty jacket and lousy but stylish dime store sneakers. She watched her stumble along, fall, stagger back to her feet, and move along again. Adela remained as motionless as possible, as she watched from her hiding place..

The woman continued on until Adela could no longer hear her, but she did not immediately follow the clumsy, desperate and obviously lost person.

She was a bit shocked herself. She hadn't seen people in months, and now there is a person near the cave. She tried to stay calm and decide what to do. Her heart was racing, so she breathed in deeply, to silently calm herself.

She carefully looked back down the road for anyone that may be pursuing the woman. She could hear her footsteps getting further away, but there didn't seem to be anybody following her. She crouched low, motionless, beneath the pines in the shadow of a little grove of mallow plants, listening and waiting.

She knew it would be risky to walk the road right now. There was no way for her to know if another person was following the woman. They could appear at any time; it could be a convenient trap.

She sat in her hiding place, knowing that this woman was in distress. She wondered, *Is there really any way I can help her?* She was in a bit of a pickle; she doesn't want people here, around her safe refuge. But on the other hand, clearly this person was in a state of great distress. Just like she had been, back in the city. But there was nobody there to help; she had to save herself, she remembered.

There was no doubt about it, she was this person's only hope. There was no one else to save her, she knew. If only she could be sure that she wasn't being followed. But she couldn't be sure; she would be taking a big chance. Something that could easily be regrettable, with the worst imaginable consequences. And then, she remembered what it's really like to be frightened and lost.

She decided to catch up to her. She stepped onto the road, quickly glanced to her left to check one last time for followers, then started a pack burdened jog after the woman.

It didn't take long. She did not get far. Adela came around the first turn and could see her lying face down in the dirt road, motionless. She walked up to her cautiously, and as she got closer, she could see her arm move. She knelt down beside her, and spoke softly. "Hello?" She touched the back of her head, and stroked her hair gently, to reassure her, and make her understand that she was being helped.

"Uh?" the woman muttered, while turning herself over to look up at Adela. "Can you help me?" she begged, a little too loud for Adela.

"Shh!" Adela instructed. She unclipped her water bottle from her belt, and held it toward the woman. "Have some water, now just a sip, okay?"

"Okay," the woman said, looking up helplessly. As Adela slowly brought the water to her lips, the woman suddenly grabbed at the bottle, and tried to pull it quickly from Adela's hand. Adela quickly pulled the bottle back, out of her hands, causing it to splash water on the woman's face and shirt.

"Hey!" Adela said, trying to control her volume. "I won't fucking help you if you don't let me!" She stood up and looked around, then looked down at the woman, wondering what to do with her.

The woman, now more frightened, scooted backwards with her hands. "What did I do? I'm sorry!" She tried to get up, but fell backwards onto her butt. She looked up at Adela with a wet face that streamed lines of dirt tears.

Adela stood above the woman and looked down at this pathetic victim, cowering in the mud. The woman returned a frightened gaze at the person standing above her.

She saw Adela as a strange, scary person, with dark eyes peering out from inside the hood of a dark green poncho. Adela's loose straggly hair flowed across her face, making her look more unkempt than she really was. Her large pack made her look bigger than she really was, and she had dead rabbits dangling from her waist that jiggled and swung with a strange suppleness, with each movement that Adela made.

"I won't hurt you," Adela said calmly but firmly, "but if you don't do as I tell you, I *won't* help you either. Understand?" The two locked eyes as if it were an affirmation of control.

"Yes, I will do what you tell me." She panted dryly, while trying to calm herself. Her breathing began to slow. She watched Adela carefully.

Adela again slowly, but carefully, held the bottle to her lips and allowed her a small sip. "Wait a few seconds and you can have more." Adela put her hand on her forehead, then held her wrist to feel her pulse. She could tell she was in a state of mild shock. She gave her more water.

Adela suddenly remembered that they were out in the open. She started to get nervous about it and tried to hurry things along.

"We need to get off this road, let me help you up."

Adela pulled the woman to her feet. She was weak but could walk. "Are you dizzy?"

"A little bit," the woman replied, holding her head with her right hand as Adela pulled her along by her left. She walked her off the old mountain road, into the wet oak forest, and down the rabbit trail that led to a nearby hidden clearing.

The forest trail soon let out into an open area, a mostly small area, with no trees overhead, but tall chaparral on all sides, making it a warm and protected retreat from a cool and dark forest. Adela led her to a relatively dry area, and the woman sat down in the grass. Adela unclasped her pack, slung it onto the ground, and then kneeled to open it. She unzipped it and produced a green, hooded, pull over sweatshirt, and tossed it to the woman.

"Oh, thank you! Thank you!" The young woman pulled the sweatshirt over her disheveled, blonde head, and then soon began to shiver, as her body warmed. "Oh my God! I was cold!" She patted her arms to enhance the effect.

"I was afraid you could be hypothermic. It's cold today…"

"Anne. My name's Anne," she offered nervously. "If you knew my name, you would say it's cold today, Anne! Right?"

Adela could tell she was frightened, nervous and chatty. You know the type, chatty when they get nervous, when they really should just shut the hell up.

"Adela," Adela said without much emotion.

"Thank you for the sweater, Adela. I'm really lost."

"I know… I know the sweater is not much, but it's all I have with me." Adela paused; she felt like she had said too much. And she probably had too. She felt like she had taken the bait, and it was beginning to frustrate her.

"Do you live around here?" Anne asked easily.

"No!" Adela said sharply. "I don't live anywhere!"

Anne could sense her avoidance of the subject. "Thank you for helping me, wherever you're from." She tried to smile but couldn't. "What should we do now?" she asked carefully, while watching Adela think.

Adela knew she had to make a decision. A tough decision.

Today started off easy enough, Adela thought while looking down at Anne sitting in the grass, shivering. *But what happened? Anne happened, that's what happened. She stumbled upon something that she doesn't understand, just fell into it. Like winning the lottery!* she thought to herself, trying to work the problem out in her mind. Of course, she knows what she could do. She has thought of this very scenario many times: what to do if you meet someone so near the sacred site.

Back before the loss of everything, if you ran into somebody up here, you would say hi and walk on by knowing that you know secrets about the place that the other person just doesn't know. But seeing other people up here was always a rare event. Cars were never allowed back here in the wilderness on these old logging roads. And Adela's sacred cave shelter was lost and known only to her father, who introduced it to Adela when she was literally a baby. They had been back to the secret spot many times together, as her father felt very protective of the site, and had worked with the forest archeologist, surveying 'off the map' sites deemed sensitive, and 'undeveloped'.

But now there is a lot to lose. In a world that has abandoned all hope, she considers this once public property, now her own personal property. This is where she makes her last stand, if there is a last stand to be made. Or at least, this is what she tells herself. This is it for Adela and the sacred site, the cave of protection and safety. A cave that has been used for thousands of years by humans seeking shelter. This is the very best that nature can provide, and she will be the very last tenant in this comfortable and sacred place.

It's a kind of shallow cave; about thirty feet deep, made of solid granite by volcanic forces millions of years ago. It's comfortably ventilated, yet the winter drafts can be controlled by blocking a narrow, natural vent towards the rear. Its entrance is wide and tall enough to walk upright through. A fine granite structure provides smooth wall space for ancient artists, whose petroglyphs and pictographs have been appreciated and criticized by art lovers for thousands of years. People who came here for safety and comfort, and liked it so much that they decorated it. It was a home; a place to return to. The ancient artists portrayed bears, snakes, suns, moons and strange geometric patterns whose meanings are lost to time. But Adela would watch them anyway, late into the evening, as they danced by candlelight and performed for her their endless stories.

In the middle of the room there were three perfectly round and smooth holes in the floor, each about eight to ten inches in diameter, two of the holes about ten inches deep, but the middle hole is twice that depth. These mortar holes were used for grinding acorns, and what have you, by ancient cooks who required these tools. It had conveniences. She would often imagine a pre-historic family enjoying the comforts of this happy spot.

The cave wasn't very deep, but at the rear of this place was a passageway that sloped up like a chimney, and if you were small enough, you could squeeze through this shoulder-wide tube and come popping up in a field that overlooks the entire mountain range. To Adela, it always looked like the top of the world, although it was only about four thousand feet above sea level. She could see a hundred miles out on a good clear day, from this spot above the cave. At night, when the skies are clear and cold, you float in the heavens and there is no separation between you and the eternal vastness of space. At least, that's how you feel.

But her favorite feature of the cave was the flat floor that led from the entrance, all the way back to her favorite sleeping spot. She always thought that this floor was a little miracle somehow, something sacred. And she believed that the ancestors of man, far back in time, also must have appreciated it for its wonderful smooth and level flatness. A feature that is rare in nature, and so nice to lay upon, and to walk on with bare feet. Adela kept it swept, and very clean.

And of course, none of these comforts compare to the hidden spring near the cave. A spring that is pure, and clear, and miraculously pumping out a trickle of fresh, clean water at the top of the mountain.

This is her last holdout of peace and safety. This is all she has left. After this, there is nothing. Nothing to care for; nothing of value. So, there is a choice to make: what to do with Anne?

Of course, she can't kill her. Actually, maybe, she could kill her. But that might be a fight, and she could get hurt. She could sneak up on her, and put a rabbit wire around her neck. That would do it. Or just a big stick to the back of her stupid head might work too. But then, she would have to bury her, and that's really a lot of work to dig a hole big enough. And who has a shovel? Then the guilt; She would always wonder, was that really necessary? a question that would be nagging her in these final days.

You think you can be a killer sometimes, but it just doesn't happen. You talk tough to yourself in the wee hours, but when it comes time to pull your pistols, you don't. You hold court in your mind, convict, then grant a suspension, give her the benefit of the doubt.

Of course, she's lost. Of course, she ran from bad people.

Adela looked down at Anne, thought her a pathetic and inconvenient sight, took a deep breath and reluctantly offered, "I have food."

Anne looked up at her. "I would be grateful!"

"I have a place. Can I trust you?" Adela was hesitant to offer Anne refuge, and she wondered if she was making a mistake by showing her the cave.

"Yes. You saved my life. I want to help you if I can!" Anne said, then started to stand up from her soft spot in the grass. "Is it far from here?"

Adela slung her pack over her shoulder, and adjusted her rabbits. She stood still and contemplated Anne. Anne began to feel insecure at the obvious inspection. "Is something wrong?"

Adela wasn't really looking at her, as much as thinking about her decision to bring her home. She was sort of looking through her, in a kind of daze. She snapped out of her deep thoughts. "No, It's not far from here. Let's go." She turned, and walked off, slowly leading the way over the deer and rabbit trails that led them through the ancient oak forest.

Hesitancy

They hiked on through forests, across roads and along creek beds, moving slow and cautiously, often stopping to listen. Anne found Adela's apparent personality and behavior interesting. She began to watch her; she observed how careful she was.

They had been following an ancient deer trace, so old and well used that it became deep, like a car tread through mud. Adela stopped on the trail and looked around. Anne could tell that she was obviously looking for some sign or trail marker. Since she didn't really know what to look for herself, she just watched Adela for some indication.

She began to wonder if Adela knew where she was going. She said that she had a safe place, but it appeared to Anne that Adela might actually be lost. So, having no other choice, she carefully followed as they hiked on. Adela stopped and turned to Anne. "It's not far now, just up ahead."

The trail continued on through the woody brush of the chaparral, and then into an old meadow of tall grass, its wispy stalks high enough to sway and rush into Anne's face, if she wasn't paying attention. She soon decided it was easier to let Adela walk ahead a few paces, so the grass could settle between passersby.

She followed Adela through a ridiculous course of stream sides, log crossings, hill climbs and unusual resting places, while Adela struggled inside with having to reveal her secret spot.

She had never told anybody about this place, and now she was taking somebody there. It was an extreme conflict that she was battling inside. She was so conflicted that three times during their hike, she had intentionally turned them around, intending to abandon the idea of taking Anne to the cave at all, and prepared a line of B.S. to explain the loss of the cave location, like: "Oh, I forgot where that place was, but we can camp here," or, "The plants have grown too high and we can't get through, but we can camp at another place that I know of."

But just as she started getting further from the cave, she would change her mind and start heading back to it, down an unreasonable, extreme and intentionally misleading and confusing path, subjecting an unwitting Anne to unnecessary hiking and physical hardship.

But Adela also knew that the world was soon ending. She had been hiding up here because the remnants of humanity were dangerous to her. *Why does evil prevail without law and order?* she often thought to herself. It didn't matter any more. The end would be soon, and final. She didn't need to continue hiding. There really was no reason to spend these final days trying to deceive Anne. She realized maybe she was being a bit manic from the whole experience. She wanted to go home, and relax, and be safe.

It would be okay, she almost said out loud. There would be no more indecision, intentional backtracking, or misdirection. She would take Anne to the cave now.

Soon they found the old logging skid, and walked out onto it. "Not far now," Adela assured her.

Anne stepped up onto the road and was a bit perplexed. "There's a road leading here? We should have taken it! Instead of walking through the stinking bushes and stuff!" She started picking twigs from her hair.

"This old road isn't passable at most places," Adela offered as a final excuse.

Anne quit picking the things from her hair, and looked down the road, then back up the road, looking for the impassable parts of the road that Adela was talking about.

They hiked the broken skid a little further, and soon came to a small rock outcropping. They walked around it and found a small opening, where the bushes were pushed aside from the rock, creating a hole between a big boulder and thick brush. The passage was kept small, so that a person could barely squeeze through.

Adela pointed to the opening and explained, "We get through here, then climb straight up, about ten feet, to the next boulder. There's a little saddle between knolls, and a flat area up there. That's were my shelter is. You go through first and I'll follow."

Anne stepped through the opening, squeezing past the brush, with her hand trailing along the smooth granite boulder. She climbed up a steep but stable path towards the second boulder that clearly marked the edge of the trail, just as Adela had said. Then, using the boulder as a hand hold, she pulled herself up to the top of the trail, and found the ground naturally level, and situated in a small forest opening. She looked to her left and could see what looked like a cave. Adela followed right behind her. "There it is!" She pointed towards the small cave as she walked around Anne.

The two walked up to the entrance and Adela slightly tilted her head to clear the five-foot-high opening, and then stepped inside.

Anne was behind her and was immediately impressed with the space. She walked around sort of pirouetting her way through, so as to take in the suitably formed, natural environment. She stopped and stood still, just turning her head from side to side with her mouth open, then declared, "I've never seen anything like this! It's really beautiful!" The cave had a small window-like opening, about halfway in, that looked out onto the path and valley below. Anne walked over to it, raised up on her toes, and looked out. She then lowered herself from the view and began to study the walls. She was amazed at the pictographs and petroglyphs, and studied them closely. She had never been so close to relics this ancient and lost. "You live here?" she asked, looking up at the ancient art and twisting her body for better perspective.

Adela thought about it for a second, and then said, "Yeah, I guess I do." She dropped her pack on the flat cave floor. "I sleep here mostly."

"What is this place?" Anne said while exploring.

"It's a cave. Just a lucky symbiosis of humanity and granite," Adela answered, doing her best to downplay her enthusiasm for the subject. "The artwork is ancient and delicate. Please don't touch it."

Anne met eyes with her and nodded in agreement. "Yes, I will respect your home. Absolutely! I'll be very careful, for sure." She again nodded, hoping to set Adela's mind at ease and hopefully gain a bit of trust from her.

"Good," Adela shot back. "I mean, thank you for respecting the art. This place is kind of special and it always has been. People have been using this space for thousands of years. My father used to bring me here." Adela paused at the thought. She quickly changed the subject. "I need to make a fire," she said. "I have a rabbit, but I need to skin it. And I don't cook in here. I just sleep and shelter here. We have to go outside to prepare our food."

"I'll help if I can," Anne offered as she watched her cross the room, and then followed her out of the cave.

Anne's Story

They walked to an area that was used exclusively for cooking, about twenty steps from the grotto entrance, behind a large oak tree. It was a windless spot, slightly cleared enough to have a small fire, and surrounded by brush. It was very close to, but out of sight of the cave entrance. Anne saw Three round stones on the ground in the middle of the small clearing, arranged around a small pile of ash. She could tell it was a very small cooking fire.

Adela pointed to a convenient round boulder low enough to sit on, near the fire. "Sit here. I'll get the rabbit. We'll make our fire here."

She returned with her small cottontail. She brought the rabbit to the fire area and began skinning it.

"How do you get rabbits?" Anne asked innocently.

Adela let out a small chuckle. "You don't get them. You snare them." She thought about it a little more. "And it's not always easy."

"Wow, that's quite a skill," Anne replied, maybe a little too nervously sarcastic.

Adela stopped skinning the rabbit and looked up at Anne, and replied in a tone that was not defensive, but slightly condescending and instructive. "You're right, Anne; producing food is indeed, 'quite a skill'." She looked back down at her rabbit, and removed the skin off the meat in one firm pull.

Anne could hear the skin tearing from the flesh, and it made her wince. "I didn't mean anything by it, I just meant that…" She paused, searching for words.

Adela brought out her hip knife and began to cut the rabbit into pieces. "You meant that you can't do it," she said, using a log as a cutting board.

"Yes… That's what I meant," Anne said apologetically, observing how well Adela handled the knife and rabbit.

"You're welcome," Adela replied sternly, whittling a sharp point on a stick, to be used as a skewer. Little white chips from the whittling flew off into the grass with each quick pass of her blade.

"Thank you," Anne said, and remained quiet.

Adela reached into her pack and produced a small flint striking kit. She piled tinder dry fibers and leaves on a piece of bark and began striking the flint, producing hot little sparks that caused the fibers to smoke. She leaned over and gently blew the smallest ember into a small flame. She placed the burning tinders between the three stones, then began feeding small sticks into the growing fire.

"Wow! That's really great!" Anne exclaimed cautiously.

Adela smiled at Anne and cheered gently. "Ta da!" Anne lightly clapped her hands and was clearly pleased. Then in a more serious tone, Adela said, "We are going to keep this fire small. Understand?"

"Yes," Anne said in a cooperative tone. By now she was learning how serious Adela was about her rules.

Adela continued, "No putting wood into the fire without my permission. We don't use it for heat or light, we only cook with it. We'll keep it the size of a coffee can lid, got it?"

"Yes!" Anne promised.

Adela again emphasized the point. "No bigger!"

"Yes, I understand," Anne assured her.

Adela took the rabbit quarters and set them on stick skewers. She then set the skewers like a little Teepee around the fire, to begin the cooking process. "It's going to take a little while. We need to thoroughly cook this rabbit."

The women sat across from each other, with the small fire and roasting rabbit between them. The flickering light from the small fire under overcast skies barely illuminated their faces in the dark little clearing. Coyotes could be heard yelping and chasing rabbits in the distance. Anne looked up and was a little startled by their sudden cries coming from down in the valley, but she felt relatively safe here with

Adela, so her thoughts returned to the smells coming from the small fire.

Adela removed the first skewer of rabbit and motioned it towards Anne. "It's a little hot," she warned.

Anne took the stick with the rabbit and began to examine it. She turned the skewer over and over, marveling at the smell, color and texture of it, and very happy to finally have a meal. She pulled a small piece from the little rack of meat, put it in her mouth, and was immediately satisfied. "This is so good! Oh, thank you, Adela! Wonderful!"

Her satisfaction made Adela feel good. She began to loosen up and smiled. "You're welcome, Anne." She paused, then quickly changed the subject. "Anne, tell me about the conditions out there."

"You don't know?" Anne replied, chewing, and caught a little off guard at the sudden change of topics.

"Well, yeah, I know. But I've been up here for months," Adela explained. "I'm out of contact. I know it was bad when I left, but I just want to know… about the conditions. Is there any order at all?" she asked sincerely.

"No. There really is no order, or law. It's bad. It's much worse than it was four months ago. Much worse!" Anne said.

Adela looked down at the fire and decided that adding a couple more sticks would be okay. She was breaking her own rule, but she wanted to encourage the conversation. "I see. Can you tell me about it?"

"It's so bad. I don't want to talk about it!" Anne protested. She looked back at her rabbit piece to take a bite.

Adela quickly reached out, and took the rabbit skewer from Anne's hand. "Then stop eating my rabbit!" she ordered.

Anne, a little shocked, and realizing that especially now, she really was at the mercy of this strange girl, did her best to defend her unintentional, but apparently careless reply. "No, no… I'll tell you! I'm sorry. That was a selfish thing for me to say. I'll tell you all that I know. Whatever you want to know." she offered apologetically, holding out her hand pathetically toward the delicious rabbit that was no longer in her control.

Adela held the skewer of rabbit, slightly out of reach, and looked at Anne with a forced smile, offering a type of contingent friendliness. "This ain't fucking New York City, understand?" she whispered at her rhetorically. Adela handed the rabbit slowly back to Anne.

Anne was baffled by the behavior, but beginning to appreciate the rare and generous accommodations. She slowly reached for her rabbit. "I do understand," she said. "I honestly didn't think I would get this far, you know? If you hadn't found me, I would be lost, or, I guess I'm still lost. But I'm deeply grateful!"

"Then tell me your story. What's it like down there? What did you see? What do you know?"

"I know that all of the cities are completely out of control," Anne said. "I think you know about the asteroid news, and how it disrupted everything?"

"Yes, I know that much."

"Well, let's see. You have been here a couple months?" Anne pondered. "So, have you noticed that there are rockets launching every day, now?"

"Yes! I see them more and more. Why are they launching so many rockets? "Adela asked, to mostly confirm what she had always suspected.

"The first colonists are heading for Mars now," she reported, "but Mars is not the only place we are sending ships." Anne explained. "Don't forget, we have a real colony on the moon, right now." She paused, and stared for moment, into the small fire. "The Mars mission is hypothetical at this point. They may not even make it to Mars."

A brief silence dominated the small clearing as they both contemplated the possibility of a Mars mission failure. "That was the very last news that I heard about space, before I started running," Anne said, as she poked at the little embers with her used rabbit skewer.

"The moon? I figured that would happen." Adela knew. "The moon can be mined, colonized, and used as a staging area for building, and launching bigger ships," she remembered. "They're using it as a low gravity space port, aren't they?"

Anne continued, "Yeah, I guess. They made such a big deal about Mars, that we all forgot that the moon is a big part of the Mars mission. So now the moon is a busy space port."

Adela sat down cross-legged near the small fire. She put a few more sticks into it, making it a little bigger than she had said that she would. She sat up straight and looked towards Anne. "So people are organizing." She thought about it, and was for a moment hopeful, but cautious. "How can they build ships big enough to transport people? And how do they keep the industry booming, if nobody shows up to work?" she demanded. "Who's building these ships?"

"Privileged workers make them," Anne said calmly. "All critical people have a chance to leave the planet before Cupid gets here. If they work hard, then they get called up on a lottery system that selects them from a pool of critical workers. The winners get the next available seats. There is no training. The workers were physiologically approved before they could work. And now it's 'go time'. That's how they select people for Mars. I've heard that maybe a few thousand people can make it off the planet before it hits. Assuming, of course, that rockets continue to be made on schedule."

It was a cool and damp early evening, so Adela put a few more sticks into the fire. The sun was low and would soon set. A slight breeze began and an occasional raindrop would enter the small clearing and land on a cheek or sleeve. The sky was darkening again and Adela knew the rain would pick up and probably continue throughout the night.

"You must have come here shortly after all power was lost," Anne said.

"Yes. Our neighborhood lost power months before I left the city."

Anne continued. "Well, of course after they announced that this God-damned global killer was to be hitting earth this December, people stopped going to work.

"I remember that too."

"Anyway," Anne went on, "there was an extreme shortage of fuel to keep the refrigeration going, in the supermarkets that had generators. Then the shipments of food stopped arriving because they were all being hijacked. Food prices were out of control and the people just literally destroyed any and all food businesses. About a week after the power loss, with no crews to make repairs, any perishable food was gone and canned food and dried goods were the new currency. After about two weeks, the cities were in total anarchy, and all police agencies simply evaporated as all the officers took their families and fled. What's the point in going to work? The world is ending!

"Eventually, the gas stopped flowing and people would simply take whatever car had fuel. Then the freeways became choked with dead automobiles and now there is no way to get through with a car.

"And today, at this moment, people throughout the world are frantically looking for food. It's all about food. Nobody cares to produce it any more because what's the point? The world is ending! In December!"

Adela nodded in understanding. "Did you work in the city?"

"I did. I was a secretary at an insurance agency in Colton. That's where I learned all this stuff."

"Where's your family?"

"I don't have any children. I never knew my father. My mother died in ninety-three, and my boyfriend broke up with me three days after the news. Fucken pussy." Anne chuckled at the thought of him.

"So why did you come out this direction?"

"Well, months after the news, I continued to work, like a good drone. I don't know why I was going in to work. I didn't make any sense. I guess I was simply in denial, and refused to believe the truth. Anyway, I made it on time, as usual. I was typically the first person there, and as I went to put the key in the lock, I noticed the doors were already unlocked. I thought maybe it had been robbed, so I stayed outside and tried to call nine-one-one, but the lines were just dead. So, after a few minutes, my curiosity got the best of me. I went inside for a look around, but no one was there. I couldn't get my phone to work, so I couldn't call anyone to ask what was happening. But in reality, I knew what was happening. And at that moment, my denial completely evaporated. Suddenly, the horror of our fate had me cornered; I couldn't deny it any longer. I felt the urge to run, to escape. But I knew there was no place to run to. So, I simply went home, feeling like I was going to the gallows."

Anne took a small bite of rabbit, and Adela silently watched her chew. Adela knew she was hungry, so she didn't protest the interruption of her story.

Anne swallowed her bite, then continued. "I stayed in my house and was afraid to leave, totally cut off; no power, phones, TV, nothing. I had enough food, but after a while I was down to five cases of power bars that my boyfriend had stored in my pantry. I eventually figured out why everybody had left. They weren't trying to hide from an asteroid, they were on the run from the gangs that were killing people for a can of beans." Anne closed her eyes and gently shook her head, "No," at the inhumanity.

Anne paused her story and had another bite of rabbit. Adela sat motionless, waiting for her to continue.

Anne looked over at Adela and could see the warm light of the small fire flickering in her dark brown eyes, as she waited for her next words. "One evening three men walked onto my porch and demanded to know where I hid my food!" She continued, "I tried to close the door but they forced their way in. I was beaten up, raped, and my power bars taken away. I am lucky they didn't kill me, but in retrospect, who would I turn to? There is no law!

"There was no reason to kill me; a witness is nothing. They took all that they wanted, then went on to the next home. These thugs didn't steal my car, because they didn't see my car. I parked down the street. So, after I got to my feet, I found my way to my driveway, ran down my street, jumped in my car and drove away. Leaving everything. I didn't know what to do or where to go, but I started seeing people stopping cars and demanding gas, food and whatever else. Then I saw bodies in the streets, and nobody was taking care of them. They were decomposing in the open. Being ignored. So, I got really scared, and just drove. I drove up Highway 166 hoping to find a solution, when I hit the traffic jam and the gang of scavengers that made me run into these mountains."

"They stopped you?" Adela asked.

"Well, first of all, you can't drive fast on any of the roads; it's a constant game of 'dodge the obstacle', potholes, cars, debris, trucks. I had to drive around a giant water tank. It was in the middle of the road! How did it get in the middle of the road?" Anne held out her arms, inviting any theories.

Adela smiled and shrugged her shoulders. "I couldn't imagine why anybody would do that."

"Anyway," Anne continued, "I'm going around all this stuff and making it down the road, when I hit the roadblock. And I mean, it's intentionally blocked. They set up a toll and were taking everything from people. I stopped about a hundred feet short of this obvious trap, and decided to back away, for sure. But when I turned in my seat to look out the back window, I saw a bunch of cars rolled out behind me, blocking my escape. I was like: what the fuck?"

"Holy shit!" Adela countered.

"Holy shit, indeed!" Anne agreed. "Then men were running out from behind those cars, so I hit the gas and went forward, but the bastards were also running at me from the block in front!" Anne paused to catch her breath. "I saw an open field behind a barbed wire fence, and I knew I only had seconds to reach it. So, I jumped out the car and just let it roll forward, then I ran as fast as I could to that fence, crawled through it, scratching the shit out of my back, and I just ran through that field and didn't look back. I heard a rifle shot, and it caused me to trip and fall, but I got up and was okay. I ran, and ran. But I don't think I was followed.

"How can you be sure?" Adela was concerned with her last statement.

Anne breathed in and let out a big sigh. "I can't be sure. But when I stopped to look behind me, I never saw anybody."

"Then why did you keep running?"

Anne blankly looked at Adela. "There is nothing left, but running. There's no reasonable argument for returning. There's nothing."

"You got that right," Adela agreed, and was satisfied with her story. "Well, you're a hell of a runner. I can't believe you ran this far!"

"Oh, I've done a few five-k runs, but never a marathon."

"That's more than a marathon," Adela corrected. "We're thirty miles from one-six-six!"

"It felt like a thousand miles." Anne thought about the distance and smiled to herself.

The girls sat across from each other watching the small fire, not speaking, but processing their situation silently, wondering how any sense could be made of their dilemma.

Anne looked across the little fading fire and scoffed at Adela with a giggle, "God damn right it aint New York City!"

The girls laughed together for a moment, then Adela replied, "God damned right it aint!" and they laughed a little more. But soon, their jovial mood trailed off to silence, and their expressions became more solemn, and contemplative. They both sat across from each other, quietly staring into the little cooking fire's last embers.

Small occasional droplets became larger, more frequent, and soon a light shower of rain began.

"Time to go!" Adela said, rising to her feet.

Anne quickly stood too. "Good timing! Great dinner! Let's go." And she followed Adela into the warm and dry cave.

Dreams

Adela lit a candle and set it in the middle of the floor, near her bed. "I have an old beat-up foam pad that I sleep on, but we'll have to improvise something for you tonight."

She went to the back of the cave and returned with eight rabbit pelts, each one about twelve inches by seventeen inches. The rectangular furs were expertly tanned and clean on the leather side, but soft and incredibly luxuriant on the fur side. She lay them out like tiles on the smooth floor, and they easily carpeted an area about two foot by five and a half feet, providing very good insulation, and a suitable pad for sleeping.

Anne knelt down on the rabbit fur bed and ran her fingers through it.

Adela handed her an extra blanket that she would use during colder weather. "It won't freeze tonight, but this will keep you warm so you can sleep." Anne thought she was being generous, and really appreciated the gesture.

Anne lay back on her fur sleeping mat and was content. Any level of comfort would be appreciated, but Adela's resources and her willingness to share were really more than she could have hoped for. She didn't really know how to thank her for such grand hospitality, so she just said it simply. "Thank you for everything, Adela."

"You're welcome," Adela replied just as simply, then laid back onto her foam cot, and looked up at the ceiling.

Coyotes began yipping, yapping and squealing at each other from deep down in the valley. Anne sat up. "What's that noise?" She had never heard such a large pack of coyotes before. The local pack had caught some small animal, and now they all had something to cry about. Their racket was now continuous.

"Oh, those are coyotes. They are harmless. We should worry if we don't hear them."

"Why worry if we don't hear them?" Anne was interested.

"Because that would mean they are hiding from something. Like a people."

"So... coyote howling is good? I mean, it's a good thing?"

"Yes. I think it's a good thing. It's a kind of warning, in a way. Kind of like a reverse watch dog; making a racket when things are right, going silent when things are wrong."

They listened as the wild canines would quieten down and go almost silent, then one or two individuals would begin urgently crying out with staccato squeals that turned to arguing as the volume of their yips, yaps and mournful, sad apologetic howling suddenly increased in volume and involved the entire pack choir, with every successful catch, dispute or random correction from their leader.

"They sound scary to me," Anne complained. She looked toward the cave entrance, then back towards Adela, who was watching the ceiling.

"You'll get used to them. They are far away right now. Sometimes they get close and it can be annoying. But they keep their distance pretty well, and are mostly respectful of my camp."

"Respectful?"

"Well, yeah, they have a healthy fear of me."

"They know were here?" Anne was getting a little nervous.

Adela rose up on her elbow and looked over at Anne. "The coyotes know everything about their territory. Sure, they know I'm here. They know you're here too. Coyotes aren't stupid. Quite the opposite. They are pack animals and they intuitively work together. They communicate with each other constantly, and it's their job to be tricky, successful and noisy. Don't be afraid of them or underestimate them. Listen to them. Trust me, they don't want to eat us." Adela smiled. "You're thinking of wolves; wolves might eat you."

Now Anne was worried about wolves. "Are there many wolves around here?"

"No. No wolves around here."

"Are you sure?" She hoped that Adela wasn't misunderstanding her question.

"Positive!"

"Whew! One less thing to kill me!" Anne felt more relaxed now that she understood, so laid back down to relax her mind. She was glad she didn't have to worry about a pack of wolves running into the cave to attack them in their sleep.

"But there are plenty of bears and lions around here, and they are dangerous," Adela added. She didn't say it to be mean, or to upset Anne. She said it mostly to just to get it out the way. She figured she may as well let her know now.

Anne's eyes widened a bit at this new information, and again she sat up. "So, what happens if a bear comes into the cave?" She was trying to prepare herself, and so now she was interested in all these new possible threats and was beginning to develop an interest in knowing how to deal with them.

"I don't know, Anne. What *do we do* if a bear comes into the cave?" Adela mocked sarcastically, and maybe giggled to herself.

"I'm asking you!" Anne replied quickly, not satisfied with her rhetorical and dismissive attitude.

"Hm, good question. Well… Stay out of its way, if possible, I guess. Umm… try to get outside? Maybe, wave your arms? Try to look bigger?" Adela giggled louder this time, and looked over at Anne, finding her reaction a little bit comical.

"And then what?" Anne's heart rate was beginning to quicken.

"Hope it goes away?" Adela really had no prediction as to how a bear would react.

"Have they come into the cave before?" Anne pleaded, as she hoped for some reassurance that they would not be visiting anytime soon.

"Not since I've been here. But I did see tracks on the road this morning. Definitely bear."

"Oh, crap," Anne said in a defeated tone. "I have heard of bears eating people!"

"Settle down, it's okay." Adela could tell she might have worked her up into a mild panic, so she elaborated on what she knew about bears.

"You probably heard about a grizzly bear attack. We don't have big brown bears around here. All the bears that live here are black bears. They are much smaller and not as aggressive. But they are still bears. These bears don't know that they can kill you, but they can. And quite easily and handily too. You are no match even for a small black bear. But our bears don't want to be around people, and they avoid us. However, they are dumb and follow their noses, which is another good reason to cook away from the cave. If you see a bear, make noise and give them as much space as you can. Let them find a way to escape, and they will. If you block them or get too close, they will defend themselves. You might think it's an attack, but to a bear, it's a defensive move."

"That's it?"

"Pretty much."

"I'm afraid of bears, Adela," Anne admitted defeatedly.

"Good. You should be. But I'm pretty sure they know I'm here too. So far, they respect this camp too."

"Thank God!" Anne had heard enough about bears. "How about lions?"

"Highly unpredictable," Adela advised clinically.

"You don't know what they'll do?"

"Jesus, Anne! They're lions!" She didn't really have any reasonable predictions about how a lion would behave either, but she offered, "If you've ever seen a house cat play, it's basically the same strategy and behavior as a lion, but instead of the cat being six pounds, its two hundred pounds and hungry."

"My cat Duchess bit me one time," Anne remembered. "That cat was kind of mean. It also scratched my sister pretty good on the leg when it was playing with her shoelace. Yeah, he was kind of aggressive."

"Right! So imagine if Duchess were two hundred pounds!" Adela chuckled. " How many times do you think she would have killed you?" she reasoned.

"Yeah, I get it. She probably would have killed me many times. She was aggressive!"

"So, imagine if she were hungry too," Adela added.

"Oh Jesus. Sure, that sounds like a monster." Anne already knew she didn't want to see a lion. Especially the creature that Adela describes.

"I've seen lion prints up here, but I haven't seen the lion," Adela continued. "I don't worry about them much because I know they don't like humans. Humans scare them. Although we are smaller, they understand that we have mysterious powers over them, and that we are the enemy. But it's not the average lion that is a problem."

"What lion is the problem?" Anne hung on every word of Adela's answers.

"Inexperienced, young lions can be bold, but mainly the older slower lions are dangerous. They get old and try for slower, weaker game. If they are injured or simply too old to hunt effectively, then they get hungry. And when they get hungry, they become a potential problem to us slow moving and weaker people. They reach a point where they are simply going to eat what they can catch, even those things that scare them. Eventually, desperation drives them to face their fears. Those are the lions that we don't want to encounter."

"But you haven't seen any, right?" Anne was hoping for a little reassurance.

Adela didn't want to tell Anne that there was plenty of mountain lion evidence in the cave when she moved in. She didn't really think it would be necessary to tell her that when she first arrived, she had spent hours cleaning up a lot of cat fur, animal bones and bits of den detritus that was scattered about the cave. Obviously, there was a lion living in this lair, but Adela thought it unnecessary to tell Anne that the big cat probably slept exactly where she is currently sleeping. No, that would just upset her for no constructive purpose. For now, she would allow her a relative feeling of safety. Besides, she was fairly certain that the lion would not return. So, she told just enough truth to be fair. "No, I haven't seen them, but like I said, I saw their tracks. So, I'm absolutely certain that they've seen me. Probably you too."

"Do you think were safe?"

"Sure, we're safe. From mountain lions." She paused, and then added, "Tonight, for sure."

Adela's information was not the most reassuring to Anne, but she was learning that in the mountains, things are very different. Life and death in this place were very close at all times.

Anne was done asking questions about predators for the night. She didn't really like the answers, but she was coming to terms with the hard truth. She rested her head on the soft rabbit pelts, pulled up her blanket to cover her shoulders and tried to relax.

They laid in their beds on the cave floor and watched the ancient images dance on the ceiling in the dimmest light of the single candle, while they slowly drifted off to sleep.

They slept well that night. The air was calm and still, and the rain was very light and occasional. The coyotes were active and vocal throughout the night and on until the early morning hours. They finally calmed down, as predicted, about two hours before sunrise. So reliable was their behavior, that you could guess, and probably be close, if you said that the coyotes calm down between three and four in the morning. Those are the quiet hours, the hours when any noise is suspect. Those are the hours when people and animals whisper.

Adela slept easily on this night. There was something about another person being present that allowed her to relax, to stay in a R.E.M. state for many hours, for the first time in many months. Anne was now a sentry who could worry about little noises in the night, and this comforted her.

Typically, Adela could easily be awakened by the hoof steps of deer outside the cave. A deer's cadence when they walk sounds a lot like the footsteps of a person. When she first heard these sounds at night, a few months ago, it startled her. She would be silent inside, listening for what seemed like hours, as the footsteps walked around the camp, outside. Finally, raising the courage to go outside and investigate, she would surprise the small herd, and they would bound away, down their little trails and traces, off into the darkness.

She was used to them now, and expected them to come through her camp every night. And when they did, although she understood this was part of their nightly routine, they would still wake her up. But on this night, the herd came and went, and she slept through their visit. And even the coyotes did not wake her, so she was able to dream. And her dreams were vivid.

In the morning, Adela was awakened by the gentle, and almost imperceptible sound of the first few sparrows beginning their day. As the gentle morning breeze stirred the boughs of the oak trees and tall bushes surrounding her camp, she opened her eyes to see the ancient petroglyphs and pictographs on the cave ceiling above her. She thought she could see them subtly move as the morning light crept in, changing their colors, shades, and shapes. She smiled at them and studied them as she had many times before.

And then, her mood became serious. Remembering her dreams, she took a deep breath and began a secret dialog in her head: *Today I must leave here. These sacred images were in my dreams last night. They told me to leave. The sun image, the bear, and the coyote and snakes. They all want me to go.*

I want to stay to defend my spring. But they said that the spring is not mine, but theirs, and it always has been. She knew this was true while she stared at the ancient art. *They also said that I will not spend my last day here. They said that there is hope, and that I should not be afraid, and will know what to do.*

Adela was saddened, but focused on the message. Of course, it was her plan to wait out the last days here. She wanted her final moments to be in this beautiful and safe place. But something was different now. She felt as if this place was pushing her away, towards something more important.

What do bears and coyotes and snakes and suns know about asteroids? I wonder if they know something. How can they hang above so confident and peaceful? Why are they not afraid? she thought.

I must leave here and learn more about their message. If I can get to the coast again, Maybe I can sneak down to the ocean and look. There must be something they need me to do! she realized.

She had made the decision. It wasn't easy. But she was listening to her spirit guides now. She thought she was doing what they would have her do. In a sense, she felt as if she was doing their bidding. She would go for them, and represent them on her final errand; this last mission to save Earth.

She reached over and gently shook Anne's arm. "Wake up, Anne."

Anne had a very restful sleep, and was quite comfortable on her rabbit fur bed. It took her a few seconds to awake from her sleep state. "What is it?" she asked in her croaky, morning voice.

"I want to go the coast!" Adela announced flatly.

Anne sat up. "It's so far! Why do you want to go? Why leave here?" she said, and then began rubbing her eyes with her fists, trying to focus in the dim light. She pulled the blanket up around her shoulders to fight the morning chill.

"We need to know more about this end of the world stuff, Anne. Something is not right," Adela said, rolling up her bedding.

"Not, right? Like what do you mean?" Anne said, scratching her head of messed up hair.

"I had a dream."

Anne was confused, again. "A dream?"

"I'm going to the coast to have a look. You can stay if you want, or you can come with me."

Anne, a little shocked at the sudden activity, and anxious to understand, threw off her blankets and began to stand up. "I'm going with you of course!" she said as she watched Adela packing and getting her belongings together. She realized she should be doing the same, but there was nothing for her to pack, because she had nothing but the sweater that Adela had given her. So, she folded her blanket, then gathered up the rabbit furs and placed them in a small stack as neatly as she could.

Adela knew she was just sitting there watching her pack, so she tossed her a length of parachute chord, and instructed, "Lash the blanket and furs together. We can use them on the trail."

Anne picked up the cord and did her best to create a manageable package that she could carry to the coast. "Is it a hard hike?" she asked Adela, in her most serious and hopeless tone.

"We can go slow," Adela assured her, "but time is of the essence!" She giggled sarcastically. She looked up at Anne. Anne was not giggling. Anne was extremely concerned that they were walking away from a safe place and into nothing but dangerous nonsense.

They stood staring at each other, saying nothing, each waiting for the other to speak. Anne's eyelids fluttered, and she had no choice but to agree. "Okay, we can go slow." She looked away from Adela and reached for her pack.

The Wave

They hiked out early that morning, while the sun was still low. The storms had passed so the day was bright and blue, with the occasional puffy cloud, and a slight southern breeze that came in almost imperceptible gusts. Adela led them on a slight detour to collect up her last rabbit snare, which she had set nearby. Anne carefully and cautiously followed her through the oak forest without really knowing what they were looking for. They stopped for a moment. Anne watched Adela look around. "Ah! There it is!" she announced quietly.

She walked over to a downed tree, then leaned over its fat trunk to grab a small wire snare that was holding a live rabbit by the back foot. Reaching to her right, she picked up a stout stick about three feet long that she had left with the trap for this very reason. She placed the stick over the neck of the rabbit between its head and body, and then stood on the stick with both feet on either side of the rabbit's head, grabbed its back legs, and then quickly and mercifully stretched the small cotton tail, breaking its neck, and killing it instantly. She kicked away the stick, removed the snare from its leg, and then gently set the soft little creature aside in the damp grass.

Anne watched the process and was a little shocked. But she had eaten Adela's rabbit, so she was beginning to understand. "Oh! So that's how you get them," she said in an enlightened tone.

"That's how I get them," Adela replied matter-of-factly. "A loop of wire across their trail, they get snared and keep pulling on the wire. It just gets tighter and tighter until they suffocate." Adela added, "It doesn't always kill them, sometimes it just traps them. Sometimes, if you want to keep them, you have to kill them yourself, or let them go."

"Why would you let them go?" Anne asked, pretending to advocate this new activity of rabbit killing.

"I'll let you kill the next one," Adela offered.

"Oh. That's okay I don't want to kill a rabbit!" Anne was sorry to have asked the question.

"Me neither," Adela confessed. "I love rabbits; they're so peaceful and beautiful. But they provide me with healthy protein, they are here year-round, and I harvest them silently."

"Plus, you can use the fur too!" Anne added.

"Sure, you can! And it makes excellent blankets and bedding."

"Oh, I know! I slept so good on those furs last night!" Anne testified.

Adela collected the trap and put it in her pack. She tied the rabbit to her belt with a piece of nylon cord.

They continued on through the oak woodland with Adela leading the way. Often, she would stop and pick up a clean, fat acorn. She was filling her pockets with them.

Anne saw what she was doing and was curious. "Don't you have enough?"

Adela chuckled. "I know, it's a habit." She picked up a couple more, then let it go to focus on the hike.

"We should reach the wave soon."

"The wave?" Anne asked.

"It's our next camp, hopefully," Adela reassured her.

"It sounds nice! Why do you call it the wave?"

Adela was about to answer Anne's question. But their conversation was rudely interrupted by the distant report of a high powered rifle. Both women stopped and looked at each other.

"Was that a gun?" Anne asked.

Adela interrupted her. "Quiet! Get down!" She grabbed Anne's shoulder and pulled her down, towards the ground, to safety.

They laid down together in the forest and listened. Another shot is heard, about a half mile away, followed up by an echo that reverberated throughout the forest, for several seconds.

"Probably meat hunters!" Adela figured. "We'll be okay If they are competent, they made a kill and now have something to do," she whispered.

They listened more. Another shot is heard, followed quickly by one last report. The nearby brush line crackled and rustled with small, frightened animals as the sharp echoes pierced their hiding places. A covey of quail burst from a manzanita thicket on powerful little wings and roared past the women, starling Anne, and even giving Adela a moment of fright.

Adela looked at Anne with a look of disappointment. "Shit!"

"What?"

"It only takes one shot to kill a deer," Adela said. "Sounds like they missed and tried to hit it on the run. I doubt they bagged it."

Anne could tell that Adela was very concerned about the botched hunt. And now she was concerned too, and very worried about the nearby hunters. "Can they find us?" she asked quietly.

"No way," Adela challenged coolly. She rose to her knees and knelt on the trail, looked in the direction of the problem and clenched her jaw with narrowed eyes. "It's a farewell party to those assholes; Anything goes." She shook her head in disappointment then looked at Anne. "Those people, that chased you?"

"Yeah?" Anne sat up, then crossed her legs, tailor-style, to better hear and focus on Adela's words.

"Well, those are the same kind of people!" Adela concluded, pointing in the direction of their concern.

Neither of them could see any distance beyond their position because they were in a very dark and dense part of the forest, but through an opening in the canopy towards the west, they could see a small patch of sky. They couldn't see the hunters, so they had to rely on their sense of hearing to gauge the distance of the rifle. Adela figured that the hunters were at most a mile away, and when she talked about them, she pointed towards the little blue patch of western sky.

Anne looked towards the sound of the hunters, and shook her head in agreement. "Fuck those people! They're fucking animals!"

Adela labeled them. "Meat Hunters!"

"Meat Hunters," Anne repeated. "Wow!"

They listened for a few more minutes, then rose back to their feet. After re-settling their packs and brushing the twigs and dirt from their shirts and hair, they continued their hike through the oak woodland.

Anne was learning that traveling in the shade of tree lines, even during the daylight, provides a type of cover, and the women took full advantage of this at every opportunity.

Occasionally, they would cross an open area such as an old road, or a meadow. They were careful at these crossings, and were quick to get through them, and quick to find a deer or rabbit trail that led back into the safety of the forest.

Adela was obsessed with the trail; she was strategic. She listened, watched, smelled and felt it. Every foot of any trail or trace that she is on has meaning to her, and she pays close attention, watching it for signs, especially when Meat Hunters could be nearby. Often, if she did not trust the trail that she was on, she would leave the trail, to follow a shadow, or take a nonexistent path that cleaved through the brush or chaparral.

Anne was a little creeped out over Adela insisting that they stop and check each other for ticks and spiders after each transect of brush parting, crawling under obstacles, and basically just struggling through the ancient thickets.

She wasn't exactly thrilled about the occasional extra effort of trail blazing, and she didn't understand why Adela was doing things the way she was doing them, but she didn't argue. Adela was feeding her and showing her ways to survive, and she was definitely appreciative of her generosity. But increasingly, Anne felt as if she was following a crazy lady.

Eventually they arrived at a ridge clearing that looked down into a small, tight, heavily forested valley. They stopped to check each other for ticks at the tree line, then crouched down to approach the ridge. The women crawled on hands and knees to the edge, minimizing their silhouettes as they surveyed the area below. Anne noticed that the terrain was very steep and intimidating. She looked at Adela briefly for clues or indications as to what they would do next, then looked back down at the thick forest, wondering why anybody would attempt to go into such an unnecessary place.

Peering down from the edge of the ridge, Adela could see the top of the granite outcropping that she referred to as 'the wave'. It was tucked tightly into the forest, with no obvious clearing around it, appearing to be just a big rock in the middle of a dense, inaccessible woodland. She produced a pair of compact binoculars from her pack and began to scan the area below.

"Looks good, Anne. No signs of people or any activity. I think it's safe," she decided cautiously.

Anne squinted her eyes, looking down at the roundish form that was surrounded by a forest of old growth madrone and pine trees. It looked impossible to get to from her vantage point. She became suddenly nervous at the idea of this turning into another dose of trail blazing. "Is that the wave?" she asked disappointedly, pointing towards the obviously inaccessible and unreachable rock dome.

"Yes, it is! Let's go down. No loud talking, okay? More listening. And let's be careful!" Adela directed. She stood up and began to walk off towards some hidden trailhead.

Anne watched her walk away. She looked down at the wave, then back to Adela walking away. "Okay, I'll be right behind you." She sighed, then fell in to follow her.

They soon found the trailhead. It was a very narrow deer trail, a small slot of parted tall grass that grew along the ledge of the ridge line. Adela pulled back the grassy cover even further, to look for indicators that this was the trail that she had remembered. "Yes! This is it!" She looked back at Anne, then stepped through the narrow passage, and they began their descent into the little valley's forested trail.

The first leg down was indeed steep, but it followed the side of a large granite boulder, so they could use that for balance on this part of their descent. Anne was preparing herself for a hard, steep slide all the way down, but she was pleasantly surprised to find that most of the trail was very gradual, as it skirted the edge of the steep valley walls.

They followed the narrow, ancient deer trace, as it hugged the steep mountain side. Occasionally, they would have to negotiate a large rock that was lodged in the middle of the path. Or step over, or duck under a limb. Or have to get around an old and shaggy trunk of a tenacious and unlikely juniper or manzanita.

There were many obstacles on this seemingly precarious trail. But because it had been used by countless deer, bears, mountain lions, coyotes and bobcats over millennia, it seemed to flow around these obstacles in a refined and safe way. Ancient people certainly could have used it in the past, and may have made certain improvements. But it is the animals who have been maintaining it, by using it exclusively as the way down for hundreds or possibly thousands of years.

Anne was grateful for the wide spots, where they could stop and rest. It was interesting to her that at these places, the deer trails would switch back and continue the gradual descent, but in the opposite direction, almost as if the animals had thought it out, and planned the trail to be gradual and easy to travel. There were a few very steep sections, but the trail was so well established from use over the millennia, that footholds were not a problem, and Anne never really felt as if she were sliding downhill, or unable to control her descent.

The trail wound through the fragile and steep forest, giving plenty of cover as they found their way through the unique and peaceful biome.

The hike down took about an hour, and finally delivered them to the tight, little valley floor. The trail leveled out and became wider, and at places, imperceptible. Anne could hear a small stream gurgling which grew louder as they approached a small creek crossing. "Where does this stream come from?" she asked Adela casually Adela, as she stood there marveling at the little flow of bright and clear water, that was rushing over the little rocky gravel bed.

"It's artesian; it's water from the mountain range."

"Amazing!" Anne replied, then stepped over the little stream, following Adela.

The path soon arrived at the cave. Adela could tell it was around noon because the sun's rays were shining on the cave site and flooding the creek area and clearings with warmth and light. They stood there and contemplated the natural structure. Even for Adela, the sight was always amazing. The cave faced a small but deep stream that was about sixty feet from its entrance. Anne could see several areas on granite rock slabs, where early natives created mortar holes. She could plainly see these work areas along the creek, and at the cave site.

She looked up at the treetops surrounding the structure, and remembered how it looked from the trail above. "There is no way this can be seen from above! It's so perfect!" she said, as she unclipped her pack, and let it fall on the trail behind her.

Paradise

The two entered the granite structure through its broad open mouth.

As her eyes adjusted to the shaded interior, Anne looked up and understood why it's called the wave. "It's like being under a big crashing wave! The roof is so smooth! Why is it like this?" she wondered out loud.

"I guess it just formed like this, millions of years ago," Adela said, squinting towards the rear of the cave. "It's another sacred place. Naturally well-hidden like my other cave, and it's a safe shelter too."

Anne walked through, admiring the pictographs of ancient animals, and the many geometrical but inexplicable designs. Adela looked around too, reacquainting herself with the setting, as she had not been here for a few weeks.

"There are many that look like people. There's a lizard, and that one that looks like the sun.' Anne noticed many round holes in the smooth cave floor. "What are those holes for?" she asked, pointing towards the group of holes, near the entrance. "I saw those in your other cave too."

"Those are mortar holes made by the people who lived here a long time ago. They used them to grind acorns."

"Dang! They must have ground up a lot of acorns," Anne said."

"Obviously," Adela replied, with a bit of tired sarcasm. She was hot, sweaty and fatigued from the hike, and not really in the mood for explaining every question that Anne had. She stretched her hands up high and arched her back, trying to stretch out her tired and pack-worn body. She dropped her arms and looked towards the creek. "I need to wash up. Get some of this trail off me."

She removed all the items from her pockets, put them in a pouch on the side of her pack, and then walked off towards the creek.

Anne watched her walk away. She didn't take the sarcasm as an insult. They were both stressed and tired, Adela's dismissive attitude was understandable. She watched her disappear around a little pine tree, as the narrow trail made a gentle turn. Anticipating the luxury of a body of water, she walked after her, with a smile on her dirt-stained face, contemplating a cool swim.

She followed the short, grass lined and sandy path as it went around the little pine tree and led directly to the widest spot on the creek. She found Adela's clothes and shoes neatly folded on a little gravel beach, so she looked for a place to pile her clothes as well. And then, there was Adela, already in the water and breast-stroking around in the cool water.

The sun was shining on the pool, and Anne saw the little sparkles of sunlight glinting on the water and bouncing their reflections upon the nearest boulders and trees, as Adela splashed around and made little swells and waves that moved back and forth, between the two sides of the pool.

Anne began to look around, and was quick to appreciate this unique riparian wonder which had, over time, dammed up naturally, forming an unlikely but clear, cold and deep pool that was suitable for drinking, bathing and swimming. It was ringed with willows, trees, flowers, shrubs and grey granite boulders of all shapes and sizes.

Most of the monolithic sized stones averaged around five feet in diameter. But one boulder, on the far side of the creek, was at least twenty feet tall. Anne thought it stood out amongst the other boulders like a king, as it reigned supreme, and surveyed its kingdom of lesser monoliths below.

Between these big rocks was a soft layer of brown granite sand covering the bottom of the creek and the shoreline, to create several small but comfortable and beautiful little beaches. Anne was so struck by the natural enchantment of the immediate surroundings that she could only stand mesmerized and watch it exist.

She was staring across the pool at a bright blue patch of lupines, admiring its contrast against the gigantic grey boulders, when a fat, black and yellow bumblebee loudly buzzed in her face and broke the spell that this place had placed upon her. And then she remembered what she was doing.

She kicked off her shoes, quickly removed her clothes, let them fall as they may on the narrow path, and was soon toes deep in the sandy shoreline. Little stickleback minnows darted in and out of her shadow, making frequency ripples to distort her reflection, as she looked through the clear pool, to guess its depth to the mossy boulders below. Her deliberate and intentionally clumsy, face-first fall into the little pond caused a big splash that made Adela chuckle. Anne's slim body slid beneath the surface, coasted under the water like a seal as she slowly rose to the surface. She rolled over to begin a backstroke, and then spit out a stream of water that went straight up like a comical water fountain. She let herself sink to the bottom of the small pool, and then began to rub her head vigorously, trying to wash out the dirt, oils and toxic particles from a week of running, hiding and trail blazing.

When she again surfaced, she felt strangely relaxed. The swim had momentarily released her from the stress of their imperiled existence. She began to stroke slowly around the pool, floated face down and motionless for at least a minute, slowly letting out her breath in streams of bubbles that rushed around her ears with a hissy, little gurgling sound. Eventually, after many savored minutes, she resurfaced.

She swam to the shallows, stood in the soft sand and wiped the water from her face. She lifted her elbows high as she swept her hair back with both hands, and wrung the water from her dirty blonde locks, while it streamed down her back and then dripped like glass beads, back into the pool, but then forming brief little puddles in the sand as she stepped onto the soft, warm beach.

As the water cleared from her eyes, she could see Adela sitting on a sunny, smooth boulder, relaxing and drying her body in the sun. She slyly admired the way her dark sepia tan smoothed over her entire body, without the tan lines from swimsuits or clothing. She thought she looked like she had been dipped in sienna paint, or like some roadside nymph statue. Her shoulder length and sun-bleached hair, atop her natural dark brown, color looked a bit un-natural, but Anne knew it wasn't. This, in contrast with her dark brown eyes and eyebrows against blondish bangs, gave her an exotic and unpredictable look. These things together, and with her stoic attitude and strict rules, made her intimidating to Anne.

Anne felt that her own skin was just too fairly complected to develop an amazing tan like that, and she wouldn't even try. But she still loved to lay in the sun, and always does, if possible. But not for long, because she could burn. So, she has to go slow; like fifteen minutes today, fifteen tomorrow, maybe thirty minutes the next, but always wear a hat. And if she were careful, she could avoid a burn. However, she remembered, there was that *great* tan that she had in Mexico, when she was on Spring Break a few years back. Maybe that was a perfect weather thing. But still, she had a great tan. It wasn't a reddish burn, but a tannish glow. A great tan, she recalled. And maybe she could still get a great tan, if she's careful.

She stepped off the beach, walked up a sandy bank, and found a relatively flat and wide boulder in the sun, a few feet from Adela. She sat down on it, extended her arms behind her, closed her eyes, and leaned back to absorb the warmth of the sun's rays.

She opened her eyes, looked around and decided that this place was a very special place, no matter what was happening in the world. The forest was very quiet but for the gurgling stream, the little birds that occasionally piped up and the continuous drone of the busy insects.

She felt at peace in this place. For the first time in a long time, she felt safe enough to relax her mind and enjoy the beauty of nature. "This is really nice, Adela," she declared, not knowing if she were even listening.

Adela was laying on her back with closed eyes. She put her hand over her eyes to block the sun as she looked over at Anne. "Enjoy it, because the sunlight will be blocked in a few hours." She put her arm back down, and closed her eyes.

Anne knew she was talking about the angle of the sun as it moved across the sky. Soon, its rays would no longer reach the floor of the narrow, and deep, little valley. She looked around some more, then lay back on the warm boulder, like Adela, to enjoy the brief, but welcome rays. She opened her eyes and gazed into the endless blue of the deepest part of the sky.

If she hadn't been lying flat on her back, and looking directly up and out towards space, she would not have seen the circling vultures. They were so high above her that they appeared as little black specks, so far away that if she shifted her sight away from them, they could be lost in her periphery vision. So, she watched the little specks circling above, trying to keep track of the little dots, high above near the upper troposphere.

She noticed that others were flying in to join up with the highest group. So, she began to count them. They found the warm thermal air currents, and were able to soar on those currents to incredible heights in their effort to catch up, and join the main flight. She watched them sail, climb, circle and rapidly gain altitude without flapping their wings even one time, as massive wing spans created a strong lift that seemed to push the flawless gliders up into the sky, in quick elevation gain bursts.

When a soaring scavenger found a strong thermal updraft, she thought it looked like they were suddenly being pulled up by strings, or taking a fast elevator up. She could see that they absolutely appeared to have complete mastery and control of the air currents. She watched and marveled at them, appreciating them for their mastery of the skies. Not rejecting them for their abhorrent behavior and purpose. She thought that at a distance, and as a large group, they were beautiful to watch.

She watched them circle above, wondering where they were off to, and why was it so important for them to all meet up there?

The little specks above eventually became a swirling galaxy of particles that looked more like a few hundred grains of pepper all circling in the same direction, on a light blue platter. As she stared at the swirling pin wheel, she forgot that they were a kettle of vultures. She watched the strange pattern as it drifted slowly and randomly across the sky.

She had intended to close her eyes only for a moment, just to clear her vision so she could continue watching, but simply allowing her eyes to close for even a moment, in her relaxed state, caused sleep to take her, and she did not resist.

They both nodded off on their warm granite lounges, lulled to sleep by the calming sound of the gentle stream, the buzzing of bees out gathering pollen, the timeless melodies of songbirds and the safety of the secret valley.

Their sleep was short, but refreshing. It wasn't long before they were both awakened by the coolness of the valley's shadow, as it gradually fell upon them. The air became much cooler, and no longer comfortable against a naked body. The women both got up, stretched and began to dress. Adela stayed barefoot and carried her shoes back to the cave. Anne was about to put her shoes on, but noticed Adela was going barefoot, so she did too.

They entered the cave with sandy bare feet, and situated a few of their items. They both put on sweaters as the valley cooled off. Anne was getting hungry, and she knew Adela was about to roast some rabbit.

"Can't we make a fire in here?" Anne asked innocently.

Adela appeared a bit angry at her ignorant question. She began waving her hand at the pictographs. "No! You will damage the images. Never build a fire in a place like this."

"I'm sorry, Adela. But the world is ending, and all this…"

Adela moved closer to Anne, getting in her face, up close. "I don't care if the world is ending! I'm not giving them up for lost! Let's just see what happens! In the meanwhile, you respect this place. Got it?"

"I got it, Adela," Anne replied defensively. "Respect! You got it! I'll be careful and respect this place."

Adela didn't reply to Anne's statement. She simply turned and walked off to light the fire.

Anne sat inside the cave and let Adela have her space. She knew Adela was inconvenienced to have another body to watch over and feed. She began to feel like a burden. She had only been with Adela for a few days , but she knew the sooner she could help out, the better for both of them. And the better to calm Adela's nerves.

Adela was preparing the small cooking fire outside, about thirty feet from the cave entrance, at a protected area; next to a large boulder sheltered by a low growing juniper tree.

Anne walked up behind her as she was striking the magnesium bar of her fire starter. Anne could see the sparks flicking into the fluffy tinder. "Can you teach me to kill rabbits?'

Adela stopped her striking. She saw that a spark had hit the tinder just right, and with a little coaxing, it could easily become a flame. But she stopped tending the fire and looked up at Anne, as its little curl of smoke gave up and disappeared. "Sure, I can teach you to kill rabbits," she said, and then resumed her fire starting once again.

"Thank you," Anne said, as if the promise were as good as the act.

Adela had the fire going between three stones, each about the size of a grapefruit.

"I'll teach you to kill rabbits, if you learn how to make and manage a small cooking fire first." She turned to her rabbit, which was laying on a small stack of broken sticks that she had gathered for the fire. "It don't make sense to bring home the bacon, if you have no way to cook it. Right? "

"Yeah. Of course. You're right, there's always more to learn," Anne offered, eager and ready to follow instruction, and hoping to be useful to this strange girl, who made excellent rabbit, and had figured out how to live comfortably in this wild place.

"I'll teach you to kill rabbits last," Adela said as she began to skin the cottontail.

"Okay So how do you start a fire?" she asked. "Do I need a fire starter, like you have?"

"Well, you could. But there are many ways to start a fire, Anne." Adela talked while she pulled the rabbit's pelt from its small body. She continued. "You can use a hand drill, or a bow drill, or a flint striker like I use. Actually, a lighter works best."

Anne chuckled. "Yeah, right? That would be my first choice."

"Well, it shouldn't be your first choice, it should be your last option," Adela said, cutting the hind feet from the rabbit, using the firewood pile as a back stop for her knife. She placed the feet on the hide.

She reached into her pocket and pulled out a plastic yellow lighter. She held it out long enough for Anne to see, then thrust it back into her pocket. "Lighters and matches are hard to come by these days," she said. "They are nice to have, but keep them for when you really need them. Don't waste them." She thought about it a little more then said, "In fact, the longer you never have to use your lighter while in the mountains, the longer you can preserve the real power of the device."

"Which is?" Anne asked.

"Instant fire, of course," Adela assured her. "An instant flame! You think it's not a big deal, but it's a big deal out here. If you need an instant flame out here, then it's probably an emergency.

"I use my flint striker to start fires. As long as the tinder is dry, I can light it with the striker. The striker works in all weather, and will last for as long as I need it. I don't worry if it gets wet. It is an endless source of ignition, but it takes a little doing, and it's certainly not instant."

A glowing object in the sky caught Anne's attention, and interrupted Adela's fire making rant. Anne pointed up. "Another rocket launch," she announced calmly, as she watched the glow of the rocket engines burning bright, illuminating the surrounding stratocumulus clouds in a pinkish glow.

The controlled explosion of the rockets thrusting engines fought gravity with all its might, and pushed its burden into heaven, with a quality of released energy that does not occur naturally on Earth.

It is always an amazing sight to any first time witness. But Anne had seen many rocket launches, and this rocket was behaving just as she would have predicted. And although she was not surprised, or startled, like she was when she witnessed her first rocket launch, the events still impressed and fascinated her to the point of her not being able to look away.

Adela also stopped fussing with her rabbit, stood up, and turned to look up at the glowing rocket climbing into the atmosphere. They watched it as the vapor trail began expanding and becoming wider when the engine flared. The first stage fell away, and drifted quickly off course with a blue exhaust trail as it sputtered out hot, bluish white dots in the late afternoon sky, on its fall back to Earth. The payload continued climbing, its contrail turning into a corkscrew shape. After a short time, it became smaller and dimmer. And after many anxious minutes, it faded away, beyond the stratosphere.

"They seem to be launching rockets all the time now," Anne decided.

"One every day since last week. Before that it was about one per week." Adela went back to the fire, sat down and began whittling skewers for the rabbit. "Something is happening, Anne." Adela started to work on the skewers, flicking her knife quickly on the stick to bring it to a sharp point.

"Yeah, they are sending all these rockets to the moon, I bet," Anne replied.

"But why? Are they expecting to survive on the moon while we get destroyed down here?" Adela suggested angrily.

"No doubt, Adela, "Anne agreed.

"If they can launch all these rockets, why can't they send nukes after the asteroid?" Adela asked.

"Maybe they are!" Anne suggested hopefully. "Maybe those rockets were nukes! We don't know what they are launching," she argued.

Adela knew she was right. She knew they would certainly be working on a last-ditch effort, even if they were currently moving people and resources to the moon and Mars. There really was no way to know. There were no cell towers active. Basically, all civilian communication was out, except for the lucky few who had CB or HAM radios, and could supply power for them. So, staying current with any information about what the governments were doing was almost impossible in these last days.

They stood together looking up at the empty sky, with its lonely, single, drifting vapor trail.

"I have a ballcap if you want it," Adela offered.

"Huh?"

"A cap. For your head. I have one you can use," she insisted. "Your face is getting red; you could use

119

some extra protection." They stood staring at each other, silently. "You will burn if you keep—"

"Okay! Okay, thank you! Fine," Anne interrupted.

Now Adela was a little confused. "You don't wear hats?"

"Yes, of course I wear hats," she insisted, repeating once more, "Thank you, Adela."

"Great. Sure. No problem." Adela went back to the rabbit, quartered it, and set the skewers over the fire. They sat down, cross legged, one on each side of the small fire, and had their roasted rabbit supper.

A Living Path

Anne was saddened to leave the wave, and its refreshing pond. She really liked this place. After last night's supper, Anne had argued briefly with Adela to stay at the site, and wait out the last days here. She couldn't imagine how their lives could be any better, under the current circumstances. But Adela was going to the coast with or without Anne, and that was final.

Anne knew she wouldn't feel safe or be happy without Adela. She didn't say as much, but she felt it, and knew it was true. So, in the morning, she woke up early and packed up silently, without further protest.

Adela figured it would take two more days of hiking to reach the ocean. She knew Anne wanted to stay, and she loved the place too. But she had a mission and very limited time.

They hiked out of the valley, but not going back up the steep trail that they hiked in on. They quietly used a trail that followed the little stream flow, and emerged at the tree and brush covered, hidden valley floor opening. As they walked out of the little forest and began to hike through the valley, Anne looked back and understood that even from this approach, that special refuge was well hidden and very unlikely to be entered by any person who was not aware of it. Its true entrance looked hostile, overgrown and just not passable. She smiled in satisfaction, believing that the wave was safe.

As they hiked along, Anne could not help but fight the urge to return to the paradise that she was abandoning, but she continued on, without mentioning it. She thought that Adela would go back too, if it wasn't for her stupid mission that was really causing undue stress in these last days. But she was sure that if she could ever return to that place, she would immediately go, stay, and never leave. She felt a strong connection to it and she kept it close, like a small, hopeful reservoir of fuel for her heart.

They continued on through the back country, trapping rabbits and eating foods along the way that Adela knows how to harvest. She had a supply of roasted acorns that she had prepared a week before, and they would have them as a nourishing trail snack, and with rabbit dinners. They would also gather pine nuts, and juniper berries when they could be found ripe.

Anne learned how to find a rabbit trail, set the snare, and then remove the rabbit if it were found dead from strangulation. If it were caught by the foot, she learned how to kill it. And Adela showed her the best and most humane way to kill a rabbit with the broomstick method, then how to safely remove the organs and bladder. Finally, she learned how to butcher it. Adela never showed Anne how to release a live rabbit. She figured she already knew how.

They were always careful to camp in an area that had plenty of cover. And they always kept their fire small, and inside the three stones. And they did not sleep where they cooked.

In the morning when breaking camp, they were careful to hide the remains of the small fire and restore the sleeping area as best they could. They did their best to leave no trace that they had stopped and camped there.

After hiking for many hours, Adela knew they were approaching a Forest Service remote fire station in the back country, so she was cautious. It was very possible that it had been discovered by meat hunters and they could be using it as camp. As the women crept through the forest, following no trail, they often stopped to listen.

The breeze was high in the pine trees and they could hear the wind rushing through. Anne thought it strange to hear, as no breeze could really be felt below, on the forest floor. A tree squirrel hopped above them, from branch to branch, chittering away with complaints and warnings. Adela stopped and looked up at the nervous squirrel. She whispered at him, but really only Anne could hear. "We don't want your nuts, you crazy little tyrant!"

She didn't expect a reaction from Anne, but Anne started giggling. She held her hand over her mouth, just as Adela turned to her and stared her down with her finger to pursed lips, silently directing Anne to be quiet.

They both stood silent and listened. Adela turned and continued the hike. Only the crunch of their footsteps on the forest floor duff accompanied them, and soon they had reached the edge of the forest, and stood under the last sagging boughs, ready to emerge onto open ground.

A recognizable sound stopped them.

"Is that a horse whinnying?" Anne whispered.

Adela could hear it too. She knew it was coming from the station. "It's a horse. We're near a Forest Service corral. Let's get a closer look."

Barney and Blue

As they emerged from the edge of the tree line, and into the clearing, they could see the cabin, and surrounding it, a horse corral, a green Forest Service horse trailer and a Forest Service truck. Slowly, they crept away from the cover of the trees, into the open, then carefully towards the rear of the small building.

Adela peeked through a back window. "I don't see anyone in there," she whispered. They walked around to the front of the cabin and could see the front door was ajar. They stopped and listened, both looking around and glancing back at each other.

Anne leaned in and whispered into Adela's ear, but kept her eyes on the front door. "Where is everyone?"

Adela shrugged her shoulders in silent response, and stepped up onto the entrance landing.

The door hinges gave a faint squeak as Adela pushed on the slightly opened door. They quietly stepped over the threshold and into a sparsely furnished room. A small table with two chairs, a single bed, and a bookshelf with few books decorated the space. A green backpack was in the corner, and it appeared full and packed. On the floor near the foot of the bed was an opened and eaten cold, can of refried beans with a plastic spoon lying next to it.

"Somebody was, or is still here," Adela said. "We should leave!" Anne, looking wide-eyed at Adela, nodded rapidly in agreement.

They touched nothing and carefully walked backwards, toward the door that they came in through.

Quietly leaving the small cabin, they crept towards the corral, where the horses were. Adela could see that the horses were on the verge of starvation. She snuck around to the tack room that was attached to the pipe corral, opened the door and could see several bales of oat hay, saddles and a room full of horse tack and horse related products.

Anne was standing outside the tack room door, looking around nervously, when she noticed that the truck had an open door on the passenger side. "The truck door is open!" she whispered hotly towards Adela, who was busy rummaging through the station property.

Adela quickly came out of the tack room and looked towards the truck. They both started walking towards it, cautiously. They could see a leg hanging out of the door.

"Hello?" Adela carefully addressed the person in the truck carefully. "We're just passing through. We don't need anything," she said calmly and reassuringly. Slowly she moved around to look through the open door.

She stepped back.

"Holy fuck!" she exclaimed.

Anne moved around to get a look too. She immediately turned away with her hand covering her mouth in horror. "Because of the asteroid? He did it because of the asteroid?"

"Yeah, probably." Adela was also repulsed. She tried not to look at his sunken face, blown in by the blast of a shotgun, or the grey matter and blood splattered on the driver's side door. They stood, staring at the grisly sight, in silence.

"Ew," Anne interjected suddenly.

Adela looked at her and rolled her eyes.

"What? It's gross!" Anne replied defensively.

Adela opened the door wider and began to take inventory. A shotgun was laying across the ranger's chest, so she reached in and moved it to the floor of the truck's cab. Hesitantly, she began checking his pockets, then removed his utility belt along with the sidearm he was carrying.

"Are we taking his handgun?" Anne asked.

"Yeah, we probably should, since we're taking the horses too," she announced casually. "But we probably don't need this," she said, as she picked up his shotgun, went to the edge of the clearing, and threw it into a nearby sage thicket. Walking back toward the truck, she met Anne's curious gaze. "Well,

I don't want to carry it, and I don't want it used against me," she explained, pretending to address the actual concern, as she walked around Anne to resume checking the ranger's pockets.

"We are taking the horses?" Anne seemed confused, but not distracted. "Why would we do that?"

"Well, we may as well take them. If we leave them, the meat hunters will get them." She found a Swiss army knife in the ranger's front pocket and handed it to Anne. "Here, you'll need this."

Anne put the knife in her pocket. "But won't the horses slow us down?"

"No, they won't slow us down, but they will make it harder for us to hide. We'll just have to be more careful," she reassured her.

"More careful?" Anne figured they couldn't possibly be any more careful than they already were. "How are we going to get horses through the forests and narrow places? It's not real..." She stopped talking when she realized that Adela had walked away, and was not listening to her.

She saw her moving towards the horses, so she jogged and caught up to her.

Adela stopped and turned to meet a fast-approaching Anne, "If they become a problem, we'll just let them go."

"Why don't we take the truck?" Anne argued.

"Trucks are conspicuous and they get stuck and blocked, and they run out of gas, and they're stupid. Were close to the coast, so why not horses?" Adela explained, pointing towards the corral. She was resolved. "I'm taking the horses."

They stood at the edge of the corral admiring and studying the sturdy beasts. The horses approached, and then put their heads over the pipe corral, to smell them. Anne backed away, but Adela stood fast and let them get as close as they wanted, to smell, touch and even snort on her, while she scratched their foreheads and muzzles. A bay horse with a black mane, and a white diamond on his forehead was especially interested in Adela. She liked him too, and she felt an immediate connection with him.

"Let's feed them. C'mon, there's oat hay and grain in the shed." They went back to the shed to gather grain bags and hay flakes. As they walked through the doorway of the tack room, they could smell the sweet smell of hay and grains in the slightly humid, sun warmed shed. It wasn't a musty smell like mere grass, but a clean smell, a comforting, warm, sugary smell, spiked with the antiseptic essence of tanned leather and saddle soap. The sweet hay bales that filled the shed with a strong perfume were packed with fructose, and if you put a piece of that straw in your mouth, and bit into a node, it would taste of the slightest hint of molasses.

She handed Anne a substantial sized flake from the bale. "Put this in their trough now, I'll bring up more." She continued rummaging through the tack room inventory.

The smell of the room was not lost on Anne; She took a deep breath of the aromatic room and remarked, "Mm, mm!, it smells good in here!" Then she walked out with the flakes held high to keep them from dragging. She wanted to push them between the posts, to place them into the trough. But the grey horse grabbed the bulk of it, and pulled it through and over the trough, scattering it onto the ground. The horses attacked the flake, pulled it apart, and began to devour it voraciously.

Adela brought out two more large flakes and placed them in the feed trough. The horses, having made short work of the first flake, all moved to the trough and continued eating. She then went to the water trough to check the water. "Looks good. They've had water; their water supply seems good."

"How long do you think they've been without food?"

"Well, judging from the ranger in the truck, I'm guessing three or four days?"

"I wonder why he didn't just turn them loose?" Anne said.

"Good question. He probably just got confused or forgot or something. Who knows?" Adela stepped back from the corral to admire the horses. "If we hadn't found them, they might have died from starvation," she said over her shoulder as she turned and walked towards the tack room.

She returned with a saddle and set it on the ground.

They watched the horses eat and felt good that they had fed them. They were enjoying their satisfied grunts and excited movements.

Adela looked at Anne. "Help me get the rest of the blankets, and that other saddle?"

"Sure." They both walked back towards the tack room.

Anne watched her with a type of amazement. Amazed that she would know what to do and how to do it. "How do you know about horses?" she quizzed.

"My cousins had horses, and I used to spend time on their ranch. My cousin Andy taught me quite a bit." Adela reached for the saddle. "Grab those blankets. And that other bridle." She pointed at the metal and leather tack hanging from a hook rack.

Anne reached for the bridle and brought it down from the wall. "So, you had cousins with horses?" Anne was a little nervous that maybe she didn't really have the experience needed to handle these beasts.

"I spent an entire summer there one year. I rode nearly every day and took care of the horses." She walked back to the corral and dropped the saddle on the ground near the first. Anne placed the blankets on top of the saddles. They went back for more hay.

"Andy knew about horses and he taught me a lot. We would ride for days through the back country sometimes. Horses are very intelligent and will take care of you if they care about and respect you."

"Really." Anne doubted openly.

"Yes. Really." She looked at Anne with a bit of disappointment at her dismissive tone, then went back to work.

Adela opened the corral and walked inside. She had a bridle in her hand and approached the dark bay that she had a special connection with. "I'm gonna call you Blue," she said, and easily coaxed the horse into the bridle.

"Why Blue?" Anne laughed.

"I don't know. He just acts like he misses his girlfriend," she joked. "I think he has a big heart." She tossed a white and green striped blanket onto his back, then went to pick up the saddle.

"What about the others?" Anne anticipated. "What shall we name them?"

"Hmmm." Adela thought, her hand to her chin as if going through names in her head. She pointed to the chestnut gelding with the blond mane and said, "Barney, for sure."

"Barney? Ha, ha! He looks nothing like a Barney!" Anne was having fun with horse names. "But I love it! Barney it is!" The girls high fived each other.

"So, which horse is mine?" Anne asked, looking at Barney and the other grey horse.

"Well, for sure, Barney is your horse." She looked over her shoulder at the skinny grey mare that they had not named. "That mare is ancient!" she said. "We can't take her. She'll have to be turned out to wander around on her own." She threw the saddle on Blue and he held steady. She could tell he was no stranger to the burden.

Anne looked at the grey mare that was to be left behind and wasn't sure if the horse was lucky or cursed. "Good luck, ole girl," she said to the grey horse munching on hay at the feed trough.

"Put your blanket and saddle on Barney, Anne," Adela suggested.

"I can't ride, Adela," Anne confessed. She stood looking at Adela with her hands on her hips, as if Adela were asking her to do something that she simply couldn't do. "I have never been on a horse." She puckered her mouth and stood looking at the ground for a moment, then lifted her head and gave Adela a defiant look, hoping that would be the end of it.

"Figured," Adela said. She wasn't going to let her off so easy. She was taking these horses and there is no way Anne could keep up on foot. She might think that she doesn't want to ride, but Adela knows that she'll change her mind quick. "I watched you scratch his neck, so believe it or not, that's the first step."

"No. I don't know the first thing about it!" Anne protested.

"Anne, the horse expects you try to climb onto its back. It doesn't know you yet. Let him know you're the boss, and he will respect you."

"But he's bigger than me!" Anne argued.

"Yes, he's bigger than you, but you're smarter." Adela grabbed Barney's reins and pulled them toward her. "See how he's willing to work with me?" Adela scratched his forehead, "He knows instinctively that I know how to treat a horse."

"How does he know?" Anne was curious about this connection.

"He knows by my attitude, my behavior and my movements." She walked Barney around in a circle. "Don't be afraid or show fear, Anne. Horses can tell the difference, just like a person can. These horses already know the rules, Anne, but they don't know if you know the rules. Everything you do teaches them about you. Be the boss. They want a boss, and if you're the not the boss, then they won't listen to you, or perform their best for you. They have to want to be with you."

Again, Adela instructed impatiently, "We have been here long enough, and had better get out of this place. So put your blanket and saddle on. I'll teach you as we go."

Anne approached Barney and walked around to toss the blanket onto his back. Barney turned his head towards her, and made eye contact. Anne backed away slightly then tried to toss the blanket up. Barney moved away and the blanket fell to the ground. He lightly stomped his hind leg and snorted, then stood still. His thick hide twitched at the haunch, at some unseen or imagined irritation.

Anne backed up. "He doesn't like me!" she said, and started to walk out of the corral.

"God dammit, Anne! Watch!" Adela picked up the blanket, walked up to Barney and tossed the blanket onto his back. He lifted his head and stepped forward a bit, but he accepted it and quickly calmed down. Then, she removed the blanket, and returned it to the ground, on the same spot that Anne had dropped it. She looked at Anne. "Do it again, Anne. Just like I did, with my attitude!"

Anne walked into the corral and picked up the blanket. Barney had his head turned towards her and was watching her every move. She deliberately walked up to him, he again moved to the side.

"Keep going! Follow him! Put that blanket on!" Adela instructed.

Anne moved in closer and flung the blanket onto his back. Barney accepted it and was calm. She began to scratch his neck. "Good boy! You're a good horse, I know. I'm gonna ride you and be your boss, okay?" Barney swung his head against Anne and pushed her, causing her to take a few steps backwards. "Easy, boy." She stayed with him, as Adela had instructed, talking to him and touching him, and slowly earning his trust.

Adela helped her with the saddle and showed her how to set the cinch straps and make adjustments. Anne watched her closely. The horses were a bit overwhelming for Anne, but she listened to what Adela said about them, and she did her best to remember the correct way to put on a saddle.

Before departing the ranger's cabin, they searched the compound for more resources that might be useful. They were unable to find any food besides the empty bean can in the cabin. Apparently, that was the ranger's last meal. Also, they went through the ranger's pack and found socks, warm long-sleeved shirts, trousers that were too big to take, a couple towels and a small first aid kit. Adela thought it would be a good idea for Anne to take the ranger's boots, because they were good boots and close to her size, but she would have nothing to do with the dead man's shoes.

From the shed she also took a fence tool for cutting fences, a pair of lineman pliers — she knew she would need these tools for cutting barbed wire fences — and saddlebags that were big enough to carry most of their gear. They tied their backpacks and bed rolls to the rear rigging D- rings on the saddle, and let their small loads rest on the horse rumps. Soon they were ready to leave the compound.

Adela had Anne help her drag out the balance of the hay and cut the baling wire, leaving the big cache of feed for the grey horse to graze on. She blocked open the corral gate so the old mare could have access to the water trough. She removed the halter that the ranger had failed to remove, and left her to come and go as she pleased.

Anne had little trouble with Barney. Although she had absolutely no experience with horses, she was able to ride Barney. He was a horse that, like Blue, had been ridden often, and treated well. Neither of the horses were too head strong, or too difficult.

Adela was able to coach Anne as they rode along. She was naturally athletic, and had very good coordination, so her learning curve was fast, and she was basically a competent rider after only a few hours of instruction. She taught her to turn him, by slight pressure from the reins against his neck, and how pulling the reins back made him stop. Anne was amazed at how gently nudging his flanks made him trot, and that pushing her feet forward in the stirrups caused him to back up from a stopped position. She was also pleased at how well he responded to touching, scratching and verbal commands. If she simply clicked her tongue, Barney would pick up his pace, and if she said 'whoa', He would begin to stop. Sometimes.

The girls moved out with Adela leading on Blue, who was understandably excited, and who tried rearing and kicking. But Adela knew that he was just wanting to run, so she let him have a little fit, and then she warned him to behave, as they left the little cabin compound through its main gate, that let out onto the old dirt road.

They rode for a few hours, but Adela grew increasingly nervous about the horses being so visible and difficult to hide during daylight. She decided that it might be safer, and maybe easier on the horses, and everybody else for that matter, to ride the mountain ridge lines. And of course, they can't do that in broad daylight. So, from now on, as long as they had the horses, they would have to travel at night, and hide during the day.

They easily found a camp with room for their mounts, in the dense cover of the forest, a place to prepare roast rabbit with roasted acorns, while they waited for the cover of night to protect their secret ride.

Descent

The expedition continued on under the shadow of a cold night, with its waxing crescent moon, on a narrow trail, out in the open and following the spine of the mountain. The ridgeline was frosty, silent and windless in the late night and early morning hours. The moon's silver sliver was low and growing larger as it slowly drifted towards the western horizon.

The sky above was dark and clear, so the cosmic display had become bright and enhanced. The milky way splashed its background of color wash across the sky, while the constellations featured the brightest stars that were arranged in many familiar, but inexplicable patterns. The starry sky seemed to wrap around the land, and even drop below their high mountain ridge path, as the sauntering group moved purposely towards the coast.

The horses ambled along, blowing warm clouds of vaporous breath in the cold, night air. They had settled into an easy and sure-footed walk along the mountain top trail, their clomping hoofs crunching away at the decomposed granite ridge, with reliable rhythm, like two clumsy un-synchronized clocks.

Occasionally, a rabbit or rodent would dart across the path. But under the slightest crescent moon, they just looked like quick shadows darting in and out of the brush line. They didn't frighten the horses, but a horse might let out a snort, or would short step, if the critter got too close.

After many long, and cold hours of night riding on the high ridge line, the flinty path began to give way to a softer soil, surrounded by taller grasses and larger, greener communities of manzanita and sage brush, as they descended into the coastal foothills.

The trail reached the bottom of the mountain, and they were soon following the course of a main coastal creek. They rode through the lush moonlit meadows that lined its edge, looking for a path to the water's edge. Eventually, they found a crossing and followed it down to a small clearing, next to the small stream.

Adela climbed down from Blue and could feel the saddle burn even while standing on the ground. She hadn't ridden in years and she was sore from the saddle. She didn't complain, but just did a few squats and twisted her body to stretch. She limped around in a small circle, obviously sore and bruised from the saddle. "Let's stay here for about ten minutes and let the horses rest and graze." She limped with Blue to the water, and he began drinking in large gulps.

Twilight had broken and was beginning to light the land. Anne could certainly see that Adela was limping and obviously in some type of pain. "Are you okay?" She was concerned.

"Saddle soreness," Adela said, pulling her knee to her chest, trying to stretch, balancing on one foot and holding Blues reins.

Anne began to dismount. "What's 'saddle soreness?'" she said as her feet hit the ground, and she tried to stand. "Oh fuck!" she cried, and limped around in a circle rubbing her butt. "Holy shit! My ass is killing me!" She dropped Barney's reins, and slowly dropped to her knees. The horse knew she was letting him go, so he ambled towards the small running stream, waded into it, lowered his big head, and began drinking deeply.

Adela, watching Anne, could feel the same type of pain that she was feeling, and couldn't help but smile a bit. "Don't sit down, Anne. That makes it worse. Try a few stretches. It helps."

She watched Barney drink next to her and Blue. "And be careful letting Barney go. I don't think he'll bolt, but just be careful."

Anne limped around, whimpering and rubbing her rear. "My inner thighs are killing me too!" She got up and walked over towards Barney. Barney lifted his head for moment, looked at her, then lowered it again to continue drinking.

"It's normal, Anne," Adela said with confidence, "It gets easier on your body. You'll get used to it."

She began to lead Blue from the creek back to the meadow for a few minutes of grazing.

"When does it get easier?" Anne whimpered.

"A couple days," Adela Assured her.

"Oh God, I don't know if I can keep riding."

"Well," Adela sighed, "we should just camp here for the day, anyway."

Anne stopped rubbing her butt for a moment, and looked up to see a flock of seagulls in the predawn sky "We must be close to the ocean."

"Yeah, we are close; it's on the other side of the freeway." Adela said. "Let's go see." She walked over to Blue. "We should get their saddles off first, so they can rest and graze."

"We can leave them here?" Anne was surprised that Adela would leave them alone.

"Sure, we can tie them off to that log over there. They'll be okay." Adela then turned, and pointed towards a small rise that was high above the grade of the freeway. "Let's sneak up that little hill and have a look."

Leaflet

They tied off their horses, and then climbed up the west side of the small, grass covered hill. When they got near the top, they dropped low, so as not to cause a silhouette, and then slowly crawled to the edge. They laid prone and side by side, on the grassy ridge, looking down onto a freeway choked and blocked with abandoned cars. The Pacific Ocean glistened beyond. Adela took out her binoculars. Propped up on her elbows, she scanned the scene below. "Unbelievable! Where is everyone? I just see cars."

"Can I see?" Anne crawled closer to Adela. She handed her the binoculars. Anne held the glasses to her eyes and could see the ravaged landscape below. In her respite from these places, she had almost forgot how ruined and dangerous the towns had become. And she had never seen such anarchy from such an elevated perspective. The destruction was so baffling to her, that she really had no opinion or protest. "Oh, no," was all she could whisper.

Suddenly, a low rumble began to develop. They both looked at each other, wondering for a moment what this noise could be. It very quickly grew louder, then near deafening, and then immediately frightful, as a very low flying C-130 military cargo plane appeared about a hundred feet overhead, traveling at nearly two hundred knots, ejecting what appeared to be thousands of paper pages. The women watched in amazement as it roared overhead, low enough for them to smell the fuel exhaust. It continued along the coastline for a very short distance, suddenly banked, and then headed inland, continuing its delivery to other lawless, and abandoned places.

The single page pamphlets had been dropped through tubes that were designed into the plane's fuselage. When the stacks of paper fell through these delivery tubes, and then hit the high velocity wind, the stack exploded into a swirling mess of pamphlets, that was immediately caught up into a trailing vortex, that appeared to chase the plane. But as the plane quickly outran the paper cloud, it stopped swirling, gave up its chase, and began to flutter about, like a flock of failing birds, each on its own individual path in the breeze, and gently falling down to Earth.

A few of the pages caught the wind and sailed over toward the women. Adela reached out and deftly snatched up a passing pamphlet that had drifted in her direction. She briefly glanced at it, then looked back at the streets below.

"What does it say?" Anne asked.

She handed the pamphlet to Anne, and then turned back to look at the ocean.

"Read it to me?" she requested.

"Okay," Anne agreed, laying prone on the ground, next to Adela. She lifted up on her elbows, smoothed out the creased corner, and tried to hold the thin page steady in the early morning coastal breeze.

"It says: 'People of the United States. A new plan is in effect to stop the asteroid threat. Please be calm and reorganize yourselves in your communities. Laws are still in effect, and there are high hopes that we can restore order as this crisis passes. We are working with our allies in China and Russia to end this global threat. Please keep faith and know that we are doing all that humanity can and will do. Food is scarce today, but know that strategic supplies are being escorted and delivered by the military to shelters throughout the United States.

"'However, while military efforts to end this threat are in full motion, remember that all military bases are off limits to unauthorized personal.

DO NOT APPROACH ANY MILITARY INSTALLATION OR OPERATION FOR ANY REASON. YOU WILL BE MET WITH DEADLY FORCE.

"'Please stay calm and reorganize your communities. Please return to your occupations so that we may quickly rebuild and recover, as this threat passes.

"'General William B. West

"'Chief of Staff. The United States Air Force.'"

Anne looked out onto the glistening ocean. The sun was rising and the cumulous clouds were taking on an orange hue. "Wow. The Air Force!"

Adela raised an eyebrow and looked sideways at Anne. She thought her reaction a bit peculiar. "See, Anne. There is hope."

"There is hope," Anne agreed calmly, looking out to sea. "I wonder why the president didn't sign this note?" she observed.

"Who knows." Adela guessed, "He could be dead for all we know."

"That would suck."

"Totally."

"What's that?" Anne pointed toward the horizon.

Adela looked out to sea and could see a convoy of dark warships on the horizon. Anne handed back her binoculars. She looked through the glasses, and could see many that were flying Russian colors.

"The Bear from the North."

"What?"

"Those are Russians. Wait! There are American ships too! It looks like they are escorting them," she figured.

"Why would the Russians come here?"

"It must be part of the New Plan that the pamphlet was talking about. They must be working together; combining parts and resources, maybe?"

At that instant several large luminous explosions occur in the distance as rockets are launched from coastal military bases. The sky begins to glow, as the missiles gain altitude, one after another, filling the atmosphere with corkscrew vapor trails, and leaving the Earth for safer planets. She looked back down on the ruined coastal village.

"We definitely can't take the horses near that town. We definitely have to go around," Adela decided. "Let's hide them, then walk down there to have a look." She looked around at the surrounding landscape, looking for a suitable hiding spot for the horses. "Maybe we can hide them in that canyon over there." She pointed to a set of little hills about half a mile away. Anne squinted to see the canyon, but really, she didn't know what she was looking for.

Little Canyon

They led the horses into the grassy foothills, where they couldn't be seen from the road.

They found a small canyon and led them into it. Adela found the location to be an ideal hiding place; it had lots of brush covering its entrance, and once inside, it opened up into a wider area, where the horses could feel safe, but not cramped. They began to tie off the horses to a large log that had probably washed into the canyon from a winter storm.

"We can't leave them here for long. Maybe an hour or two."

"That's not much time!" Anne said, then rephrased her statement. "Is that enough time?"

"We're going for information," Adela said, "Let's just go in really quick and see if we can get more info."

"What kind of info?" Anne asked, wondering if there was some way to talk her out of it.

Adela stopped fussing with the horses and turned to Anne. "Any information, Anne!" Adela's patience was wearing thin on the subject. "Anything about the launches, or the asteroids, or anything about this fucked up world!"

"Well, it will take us at least a half hour to get to the freeway from here, and then another half hour to walk into town," Anne advised guardedly.

Adela knew she was right, and that the horses could be here in this canyon, if they don't get loose, for many hours. And if something went wrong, the horses could be stuck there for days.

"Yeah, yeah. I know. But let's do our best to get back as fast as we can" She re-checked the horses' ropes to make sure they were safe. She hoped that they wouldn't chew through them during the coming long hours, tied up to a tree branch in a small hidden canyon. "Tonight, when we get back, we can take the horses down the creek, under the freeway, then onto the beach." Satisfied that the horses were secure, she picked up her pack. "Let's go."

As they walked out of the canyon, they carefully placed scrub brush across the path to hide the entrance. Adela used a switch of brush to sweep their foot and hoofprints from the trail, hopefully removing any clues that could betray their hidden corral.

Footprints

The meat hunters found the Forest Service cabin on a four-wheel utility ATV. They had been out hunting all morning, and had seen no game, but had stumbled upon the compound.

Fuel was extremely hard to come by, and they didn't have much left in their dented gas tank. It wasn't too difficult for them to get this far back into the mountains and haul game on the old quad. But this vehicle did have its problems: its cylinders were not firing correctly due to dirty spark plugs. It was constantly used, never maintained, and frequently over-revved. And because of this, it began blowing smoke from leaky piston rings that were prematurely worn from an overheated engine with a chronically low oil level.

They pulled into the yard on their smoking and sputtering ATV and shut down the machine at the front door of the cabin. Two men with rifles slung on their backs stepped off their ride and began to look around. They both spun around in their tracks, trying to decide which area to clear first.

They had beards, dirty and torn clothes, and ball caps. The man wearing the green John Deere cap and dark tear-drop Aviators looked towards the open corral, and the fresh hay piled near the tack shed. "Bet these are the horses that left those tracks that we saw on the way in."

His partner, wearing a torn red and blue shirt, and a dark blue cap with a sheriff's insignia on it, replied, "Yup, those are hoof prints. This place had a bunch of horses, and not too long ago, neither." He nudged his partner with his elbow and pointed. "Hey, Larry, there's a truck over there!" He started walking towards it hoping to find its tank full of gas.

"It's diesel, Charlie," Larry yelled back, then he too began walking towards the truck, regardless. "We need gas!"

They walked to the truck's open door and found the ranger on the front seat of the pickup.

"Son of a bitch!" Larry declared, lowering his sunglasses to get a better look.

"Holy shit!" Charlie agreed. "Looks like they killed him and robbed him!" He instinctively turned around and quickly surveyed the surrounding yard, wondering if the killer was still nearby.

"Maybe." Larry wasn't so sure. He checked the ranger's pockets and could see that they were turned out and empty. He held up the empty gun belt, saw it was worthless to him, so he let it drop to the cab floor.

"Whoever they are, they have a shotgun. Doesn't Rex use a shotgun?" Charlie suggested, referring to another meat hunter who both men know to be ruthless and cruel.

"Naw. Rex didn't do this. Besides he rarely leaves the foothills." He began looking around on the ground. "That is almost certainly a woman's footprint!" He squatted down and inspected one of many prints that Anne had left with her sneakers. "This other shoe... Hmm, could be a girl too. Or a guy with small feet."

Charlie also squatted down to inspect the prints. "Yeah, they are kind of small."

Larry stood up, looked around, then headed for the cabin. He walked up to the cabin door and shoved it open with his foot. Leading with the point of his rifle, he entered quickly. Charlie was right behind him.

Inside the cabin, they found a backpack that had been rummaged through. The bed was covered with various items and a few clothing articles. One of the items was Anne's old blouse. Larry picked it up and smelled it. He held it out and could see it had rips, and was scuffed and dirty. He looked at Charlie, grinned, and shook his head to confirm, "A girl was here all right." He picked up a pair of the rejected trousers, then tossed them back on the bed. "Either these pants were too big to take, or too small. If I were to guess, judging from the footprints outside, these pants were too big for either of those people. I bet they are both women."

"I'll be damned!" Charlie realized, "Girl killers, whoa!" He started to chuckle.

Larry kicked at the can of beans on the floor and it spun across the room and bounced off the wall. "Let's look in that shed, out back."

The men stomped out of the cabin and walked briskly to the shed. The door was wide open. Larry looked inside and found no saddles, but he did discover a pack frame and another bridle and harness. He walked out and looked around. He could see a horse trailer behind the shed, but no horses.

"They definitely took some horses," he decided, and went to the ATV. He slung his rifle across his chest, then climbed on. Charlie sat behind him, while he started up the weak engine. Blue smoke popped from the dingy tail pipe, as they drove away, slowly, following hoofprints.

A Walk into Town

The women walked out of the foothills and eventually found themselves once again at the ridge overlooking the freeway. They scanned the mess below. Adela knew there was no safe way into this city. For the most part, the streets looked like abandoned traps; blocked with cars, trucks, trailers and many objects that been dragged or dropped onto the former roads.

They descended down the hill, following no trail, but transecting a straight line through the overgrown grass and weeds. Emerging onto the roadway, they stood amongst the broken vehicles.

Both women were scared, but Anne owned it. She grabbed Adela's arm and held tight. Adela tried to shake her off, but Anne wouldn't let her. As soon as Adela broke free, Anne would grab her again and find better ways to hang on to her. So, she gave up, and just got used to Anne being there.

They started walking through the car graveyard, carefully exploring and looking behind themselves. The cars were so hopelessly packed in that often they had to climb up onto the hood of a car, then step from car to car. Having reached the other side of the jumble, they climbed down, onto sidewalks that were strewn with trash and consumer items of all sorts; furniture, plastic, bedsprings, car parts and innumerable pieces of consumer detritus. The sidewalks and roads were now, literally, dumps.

There were buildings here, but not many people. Occasionally they would see a person scavenging, looking for food. Probably looking in the same places over and over again.

They kept moving, not finding a safe passage, and beginning to feel remorseful about coming here.

As they advanced through the garbage strewn world, towards an abandoned shopping center, they realized that a very desperate and malnourished man was walking towards them. They stopped, and cautiously let him approach. He was very thin and his cheeks were sunken and hollow. He fell to his knees, but shakily rose back to his feet, walked towards them, and stopped about ten feet away. "Do you have any food?" He stared at the girls, as if simply focusing on them was an effort.

"No. I'm sorry. We have no food," Adela answered quickly.

Anne looked at Adela, and Adela knew what she was thinking. So, she looked back at Anne, and gave her the 'look'. She turned back to the starving man, and slowly shook her head, no.

"Not for me." He smiled weakly. "For my daughter and my wife." He turned and looked towards a woman and child standing off in the distance.

Adela could see them standing by a looted, wrecked truck, about a hundred yards away, distant silhouettes of windblown hair and tattered dresses. The girl wanted to wave, but the mother reached for her arm and held it down.

Adela knew that this man was desperate. She knew that these people were starving to death. She had food, of course: rabbit meat and roasted acorns. And Anne knew it too. Anne knew she had three packages. Each package had a meal's ration of smoked rabbit and roasted acorns. But Adela also knew, that even if there was enough food to go around, people would want to know where it came from. She felt that her safety depended on her keeping these secrets.

"We have no food either. We are here looking for food," she lied.

The man looked at Adela with a pitiful look. "There is no food here. Some people get food, but not us." He started to turn away.

"Wait!" Adela walked towards the man. "What do you mean 'some' people?"

He stopped and turned around to face her. "Hunting gangs. The gangs eat."

Adela knew who he was talking about. "Don't they share with people?" she asked.

The man managed a weak, fake laugh. "They would kill you for asking." He slowly shook his head. "No, food is currency. It cannot be bought. It can only be only earned."

"How do you earn food?" Adela asked.

The man paused and took a deep breath, trying to find the words to answer the question.

Finally, he said, "I try not to think about such things, ma'am."

He stood there looking at her, thinking how beautiful and healthy she looked. Wondering where with this young woman would be if things were different. He smiled at her.

Adela smiled back. "Where is everybody? Are they hiding? "

He looked towards her vacantly. "I don't know, we arrived three days ago and the city was empty." He lowered his head, defeated that there was no food.

Adela felt trapped by his presence and could tell Anne was anxious too. She made her break. "We must be going. Good luck, sir." The girls walked around the man and swiftly continued towards the shopping center. They walked about twenty yards from the man, when they heard him shout weakly, "There's nothing there!"

Adela stopped and turned around, facing the man. She removed her pack, opened the top flap, took out a ration of rabbit and roasted acorns, wrapped in paper tied with string, and set it down on the ground.

He watched the act and started walking towards the gift. The girls turned and marched away.

"Thank you!" he cried weakly after them.

They quickened their pace.

Their arrival at the coastal shopping center was also an extreme, and regrettable disappointment. It looked dangerous. The parking lot was littered with broken vehicles, garbage, shopping baskets and the occasional corpse.

There was nobody burying the dead. Even on the coast with prevailing winds blowing against the coast, the city still stunk of garbage and rotting flesh.

This used to be a premier commercial area on the coast, but now? No. Now it's a waste land. This small town was stripped clean of all food months ago.

But where are the people? Adela thought to herself. She looked around and could see houses up on the hills. She knew there were neighborhoods of homes nearby. She knew that if any people were left, they were hiding.

A loud scraping sound on the pavement got her attention. She turned toward the sound, and so did Anne. They saw a couple moving an upturned shopping cart away from a pile of cardboard.

The man saw the women and immediately hailed them "Hey! You got any food?" he shouted, then began climbing over debris, and around dead cars, to get to them. His woman partner followed up, as fast as her limping and malnourished body would allow.

Anne and Adela began walking faster, but not fast enough. The man ran up behind them and grabbed Anne's shoulder, turning her around, knocking her off balance, and pushing her to the ground. "I don't, I don't have any food!" she cried "Please don't!" She held her arm over her head, as the wretched man tried to remove her pack. He was pulling on the straps, and dragging Anne through trash and mud, jerking at her pack with a dog-like rhythm, grunting with each angry tug.

Adela ran at him and rushed into him with all her might, crashing her elbow into the side of his head, and forcing him to release his hold. He fell off Anne and into a scattering of broken glass. Adela grabbed Anne's arm and pulled her to her feet.

The man stood up and twisted his arm to get a look at his now bleeding elbow. He redirected his attention back at Adela, as his weak companion walked up behind him. "Give me your fucking food!" He stood panting, then advanced two steps as Adela brought up the ranger's pistol. The man stopped. "You gonna kill me? Over food?"

"Just let us go, Mister! I don't want to hurt you!" she said, pointing the muzzle at his mid-section. She was unsure if the gun safety was on or off, or if the gun would even shoot. She tilted the gun slightly to look at the safety, and the man saw the look.

He thought he could see the doubt and fear in her eyes. He could tell that maybe she didn't really know about the gun, or maybe, she didn't really know how to use it at all. She certainly didn't look like she knew what she was doing, holding the weapon one-handed, with her left hand straight out from her side, like she was reaching for some invisible thing to hold on to. And truthfully, she couldn't decide whether to break and run, or stand her ground and make him back away. Oblivious to her own almost comical, yet amateurish handling of the weapon, she held steady, with it trained on the belligerent and persistent scavenger.

Anne stood frozen, behind her, hoping the man would heed the warning, and go away.

The starving man's companion stood watching, delirious and worthless. "Can we have some food?." she said, not caring, or forgetting about his talk of death, apparently oblivious to the levity of the situation. "Do you have food?"

"They have food, he said." He pointed at them, "Look how full they are!" He looked over at his companion in a way that Adela instinctively felt was an indicator of his imminent attack. He lunged at her and tried to close the six-foot span in one step. But by the time he had reached her, she had fired three shots into his torso. He fell towards her, but was unable to grab at her. She stepped to the side and he collapsed at her feet, as brass casings bounced around, and made little chime like melodies against the asphalt road.

Adela's heart was racing and she began to panic. She turned and ran towards the freeway, Anne following as fast as she could go. The man's companion walked over to him and simply looked down upon his failed effort. She turned and slowly shuffled away.

They ran through the trash riddled streets, then climbed hood to hood until they reached the freeway, and their entry point. As they started to climb up the steep embankment, they heard shouts and laughter. "Get down!" Adela warned, and pulled Anne to the ground, behind a mass of stalled cars.

They crouched hidden from the approaching gang, and clearly could hear a horse's hoof steps clipping down the pavement. Adela was horrified at the sound. Her first thought was that they had found the horses. She slowly crept up, and peeked over the hood of the wreck that was hiding them. She quickly lowered back down and turned to Anne, "They got the grey!"

Adela began to cry, "We shouldn't have turned her out!" she whispered, her whimpers louder than her voice. "We should have taken her!"

Anne consoled her. "We've still got Blue and Barney hidden, Adela. We saved them, at least."

The gang walked on by with the grey, to prepare a guarded and privileged feast. Anne tried to rise up for a look, but Adela pulled her down. "No! Stay down!"

The girls sat hidden and waited until the hunting party had long passed. Hoping the gang was long gone, and that nobody was looking, they hurriedly climbed the embankment as fast as they could. They reached the top, crossed the jumble of broken cars on the freeway, and quickly slid down the wide shoulder to the bottom of the mountain side embankment. Adela cut the fence, and they rushed onto the grassy pasture lands of the coastal foothills.

Good Horses

They impatiently hiked back to the horses, but cautiously approached, as they got nearer. They stopped to listen. They heard a snort. Adela smiled at Anne and they continued forward, found the covered entry, removed the brush, and found Barney and Blue standing where they had left them.

They walked into the little canyon and up to the horses. Blue and Barney seemed unconcerned and patient. "These are good horses," Adela said.

"Yeah, they are," Anne agreed.

"I think we should stay here until tonight." Adela looked around. "It seems really safe and hidden here." She placed her pack on the ground and looked around for three round stones to use for the cooking fire. "I set a trap out near the road this morning. Looked active. Pretty sure there's a rabbit there." She started walking away. "Be back in a few minutes."

Anne stood next to the horses and watched her hike off. She shook off her pack, and let it fall to ground behind her, then sat on a big flat boulder. Waiting.

Adela returned with a cottontail. She walked over to a clear area that would be suitable for a small fire. She held the rabbit close, wrapped in her arms, as if it were a child, and then fell to her knees. She began to cry big sobs of sincere grief into her little armful of soft fur. Anne approached her carefully. "We couldn't have saved the grey, Adela. There was nothing we could have done."

"Fuck the grey, Anne!" Adela corrected. "I don't care about the grey. It wasn't his fault! He was starving. And I killed him!" She wiped her face with her sleeve, and then cried some more. The rabbit fell to her lap, and then rolled onto the ground.

Anne stood above her and said nothing more. She picked up the rabbit, walked out to the trail and removed its entrails with her knife. She dumped the guts over the side of the small path and returned to the fire area. Placing the three stones that Adela had found in a small circle, she gathered nearby dead brush and piled it between the three stones. Then she asked Adela for her lighter. "Let's make this easy," she requested. Adela casually handed her the yellow lighter, without hesitation.

Anne lit the small fire and placed small broken branches in it to get some coals and heat going. She skinned the rabbit, cut off its feet and head, then quartered it, and set the pieces on skewers that she had quickly whittled from little green willow branches.

The rabbit was cooking over the fire. Adela could smell the roasting flesh as she leaned back, and watched Anne prepare their dinner.

They had their meal and soon dozed off, around the little fire, while the horses stood patiently and quietly throughout the evening.

Adela awoke a few hours later to put grain bags on the horses. It was cool this evening and she decided the comfort of a small fire would be helpful. She began stowing her gear, when Anne woke up. She sat up and yawned. "What time do you think it is?"

Adela looked at the stars. "I'm guessing ten? Eleven?"

"Hm, its cold," Anne said.

"Yeah, you'll warm up on Barney. Let's get 'em saddled up, and head for the beach," Adela suggested.

The sky lit up, as another rocket from the Airforce base was launched, and rumbled away.

The girls would occasionally glance up at it as they put blankets and saddles on Blue and Barney. By now they were used to rocket launches, so they didn't really discuss it much in detail any more when they occurred. "That's nine since this morning," Anne observed.

"Yup, they must be busy over there."

The packs were secured on the horse's rumps, then they saddled up, and rode out of the little canyon.

Crossing

They returned to the stream that flowed under the freeway. They rode beyond the crossing where they had last watered the horses, and followed the meadow to get closer to the freeway. Adela got down from Blue, produced her lineman pliers, and cut away strands of barbed wire fencing that were blocking their travel. She pulled the loose wire back as far as the post would allow, then wrapped the wire on the lowest strand to keep it away from their path.

By the time they had reached the creek at the point where it went under the freeway, they had cut the fence five times, and left the breaches open, remembering the route. They both got down from the horses to let them graze in the meadow for one last meal, before riding the beach.

They held their reins as they watched them munch on the fresh grass. "How's your butt?" Adela asked seriously.

"Better," Anne said with a half-smile. "Still sore." She rubbed her butt again. "But I'll live."

Now, Anne was beginning to get more concerned. She didn't really understand why they were even here. She trusted Adela to a certain extent, but the more she thought about what they were doing, the less sense it made to her. "So, um, where are we going?" she asked cautiously, and at a time in the game when turning back was out of the question.

Adela bucked the inquiry, and simply changed the subject. "We should saddle up soon, Anne. We need to follow this creek under the freeway, and get onto the beach."

Anne needed answers. "We came here for information, we got a little bit, I guess. So, let's go back now. This place is unsafe, Adela!" She was scared, and Adela could feel her fear. She was hoping that Anne would not become uncontrollable somehow, or become an annoying distraction.

"It's, okay, Anne. I just need to get down that beach, and be near those rockets. That's all I'm doing. It's all I want to do." She looked at the stars, then back at Anne.

"But why? Why is my question to you! Why must you be there?" She stood waiting for the big reveal.

"To pray."

"What?" Anne was quick to be furious. "Why the hell can't you pray up in the mountains?" She crossed her arms and took a short walk, then turned and quickly walked back towards Adela. "Why the beach?" she growled.

"It's not just the beach, but where the beach takes us," Adela replied calmly.

"And where is that?"

"The Air Force base." Adela reached for Blue's saddle horn, and lifted her foot to the stirrup. She was still a little saddle sore, but pushed through the pain and was able to throw her leg over his back and get back in the saddle.

"Oh really?" Anne replied sarcastically, looking up at Adela, who was now shifting uncomfortably on Blue. "You mean the same Air Force base that the flyer warned us to stay away from?" She looked at Adela with an incredulous expression.

"Yeah, that's the one!" Adela replied quickly. "C'mon, mount up!" she said confidently, completely dismissing Anne's obvious concern.

"No!" Anne stood fast. "I'm not going near that Air Force base! They said they will shoot us!" Anne was beside herself, contemplating a suicide ride.

Adela looked down at Anne. "You can go back if you want, but I know those meat hunters who took the grey are out there too. I brought you with me because I felt I had no choice. I could have left you in the mountains to starve to death, but I didn't. So, you're here now. If you come with me, you won't be alone, and neither will I. And I feel like I need you with me on this last mission."

"Mission?" Anne shook her head in frustration, "This is a mission? To accomplish what?"

"I told you: to pray. I want to be close to the rockets, to see them, to support them."

Anne was at a complete loss. Nothing that Adela was saying was really making any sense. She was sure that Adela had lost it. "I'm terrified to be alone out here, Adela. I'm really scared. But I don't want to be killed by soldiers either!" Tears were forming in her eyes. She knew she could not convince Adela to turn around.

"We're going to die soon, Anne…"

"Maybe!" Anne interrupted. "The flyer said they are working on it!"

"I understand all that, Anne. But this world needs all the help it can get. This is not the time to do nothing and just 'see what happens'. This is the time to act. I'm going to do something; I'm not just going to accept the military's word; I'm going to make an effort too. And the last thing I'm going to do is to pray for wisdom, and meditate to help guide our rockets. I need to know what type of rockets they are; I need to know what they look like. I need to be near them!"

"That's ridiculous." Anne sat down in the grass. "Did you pray for all the rockets that have left so far? All those rockets that we have been seeing, daily. Did you pray for them?" She cried, in a mocking tone.

"Yeah, I did," she confirmed.

"I didn't notice," Anne scoffed. "So, why is that any different?"

"I don't know," Adela confessed. "It's like a mecca for me. I need to go there. I'm going there."

"I didn't realize that you're so religious."

"I'm not, really."

"Then why are we doing this?" She was really hoping for the smallest shred of reason. Adela looked up at the sky, searching for an explanation that Anne may understand.

"Well, hmm, let me see… It's like this: I believe that I can appeal to the universe, this end. Maybe I can help change it. Maybe the source of all this doesn't know my position on the subject. I think I have a convincing argument."

Anne thought her explanation was completely delusional. "Oh, I see. Like *Horton Hears a Who*?" Anne let out a contemptuous huff and looked away.

"Sure, use that analogy if you like."

Anne summed up the impossible mission. "This is suicide, you know. We will be killed."

"Maybe, but…" Holding the saddle horn, Adela leaned over to get nearer; to emphasize her point. "This is the last battle to save Earth, Anne. Don't you want to be part of it?" She sat up straight, then stood in her stirrups to ease her sore rear end. "You have nothing to lose, Anne," she reassured her.

Anne stood up, feeling defeated, and went to Barney. She took up his reins, put her foot in the stirrup, and then pulled herself onto his back. She pulled Barney's reins to the left and he twisted his head left, following through with his huge body. He described a small, tight circle as he turned around, and then quietly followed Blue down the small path that led into the creek.

The trail that went down into the creek was very narrow, and rarely used by any animal bigger than a deer. They dismounted and led the horses along the dark and damp path. Adela brought out a small flashlight that she found in the ranger's pack. She was careful to keep the beam pointed down, and only use the light in quick bursts, at places where she absolutely could not see.

The dark little trail crossing soon opened up with the tunnel opening to the right, and the small trail continuing into it. The six lane, flood control tunnel had a fair amount of debris scattered throughout, from the last storms; mainly tree limbs and trash. Adela pointed her light above the waterline and saw a trail that led above the creek and alongside the gigantic bridge footing.

They walked in front of the horses, leading them into the tunnel, and up and onto the more elevated concrete path. The saddles and packs scraped along the wall of the narrow passage, as they carefully stepped through the dark and unpredictable course. There were two large boulders that the horses had to step onto to get over, and the girls had to move an old rusty and crumpled washing machine out of the way and send it tumbling into the creek, but they were able to eventually get through.

They emerged from the tunnel to find themselves on the beach side, but facing yet another obstacle. They had successfully avoided going through the town above, but now they had to cross a small lagoon.

The surf had created a sandbar at the mouth of the creek and as a result, a large pond had formed at the outlet of the waterway, before it ultimately spilled into the Pacific Ocean.

They stood with the horses on the creek bank, looking at the other side. "We need to mount up." Adela turned to Blue, and climbed onto his saddle. "If we hit deep water, don't panic, and let Barney swim; don't pull his reins, okay?"

Anne had mounted Barney and was looking at the pond, contemplating the deep water.

"I'll do my best," she promised. "Anything else?"

"Yeah, if it gets deep, just hold the saddle horn and let him pull you through the water. Don't try to sit up high; try to get your weight off him. Don't drag him down!"

Anne sat waiting for Adela to go first.

Blue stepped into the creek, wading into knee deep water. He walked out about twenty feet and then found the channel. He sank down into the deep crossing and bobbed up and down a few times before realizing he must swim. His long legs pulled small hoofs through the water with surprising efficiency. As his body sank into the dark crossing, Adela let herself go prone and be pulled along, taking her weight off of his struggling back. Anne watched the demonstration, and then began her crossing.

Barney splashed into the creek and without hesitation followed Blue's path into the deep channel. Anne was surprised at how powerful a swimmer he really was. His head briefly slipped under, but he lifted it high and snorted loudly to clear his nostrils. She realized she was pulling him down, so she held his saddle horn, and let the weight of her body float behind them. His swim strokes were now steady and forcefully effective, and he easily pulled them quickly to the other side.

As Barney began to find footing on the other side of the channel Anne quickly pulled herself back into the saddle before he found traction, and when he did, he began lunging, with shockingly energetic thrusts, to get into the shallow water. She hung on with all her agility, and let him hop and lunge, as he doggedly brought her up, and delivered them onto the beach.

The riders faced each other, each waiting for the other to comment first, as they sat on completely soaked, dripping horses who were snorting, switching their wet tails, shifting nervously, and glad to be on dry land.

Barney coughed a few times, and the crossing was done.

Beach Ride

They began riding southwards on the deserted beach. The moon was approaching its first quarter and spilled little light. Adela thought it was too much light, but she was glad it wasn't any brighter. A light mist enveloped the surf line, as the big rollers broke and blew damp pockets of cool air towards the shore.

The coastal town above was dark, and as they rode along, they looked up and could see the occasional flicker of light from a candle, or fire. And if there were any people living up there, they could not be heard or seen. Maybe they were watching, but if they were, they did it from a hiding place.

After a few very tense miles of sneaking by the town, the landscape opened up leaving the town behind. To their left were vast sand dunes that went far inland, and on their right was the Pacific Ocean. The tide was beginning to go out, so the horses had plenty of hard packed sand to comfortably tread on. They moved easily through the night, getting ever closer to the forbidden zone.

Adela noticed a bright, white pinpoint of light amongst the stars; quickly it grew into a bright orange spot. Then another point of light grew. Then more followed. She counted seventeen in all, all exploding in sequence, one after the other, then slowly going dim, like stars being born and dying in a matter of minutes. The girls stopped, and watched the display.

"I think those are nukes!" Adela said joyfully. "They must be hitting it with nukes!"

"Oh good, good!" Anne rejoiced. "Please work, please work, please work!" she cried.

Adela looked at Anne and asked, "Who you praying to?"

Anne laughed. "Good one! Got me!"

"Who?" Adela insisted.

Anne knew she was being hypocritical. "Whoever will listen, I guess. I'm allowed to hope!" she protested lightly.

As they turned away from their distraction and again headed south down the beach, another rocket was launched. They were close now, and could hear the distant rumble of its massive engines pushing the payload into the heavens.

"How much further? Anne asked,

"About five miles to the barrier." Adela nudged Blue and he broke into a canter.

Barney, without much coaxing from Anne, quickened his pace as well. "The barrier?" she asked after her, but Adela either ignored her, or could not hear, so Anne caught up to her and ran along side.

"The barrier?" she repeated, over thumping hoof beats pounding out a sandy gallop'

"Yeah!" Adela said in a raised tone, loud enough to hear over the rushing wind and pounding surf. "The barrier is the point were not supposed to cross. It's a big fence that keeps people out."

"Oh good!" Anne replied in a relieved tone. Relieved that there was a barrier, and hoping it was enough to keep Adela back and safe. She imagined they would stop there.

Adela slowed Blue down to a walk. Anne also slowed down and things got quieter, and the horses calmed down. "They wanted to run," Adela said.

"I could tell," Anne replied. The horses walked along at their nice steady gait. The girls kept them calm and let them find their own comfortable pace, to cover the remaining miles.

As they got nearer to the barrier, they encountered many broken and burned-out automobiles. There was much trash, and personal belongings scattered about. It looked like a small war had occurred, and they were riding through the resulting destruction. They tried to not look, or comment, when they found several dead bodies that looked like civilians, washing back and forth in the surf line. They simply rode past them.

Anne was not as terrified as she would have been a few weeks ago, before she met Adela. They had been through several terrifying ordeals together, but this was different. This was terror on a much larger scale. Anne tried not to process the scene, but to simply ride through it and avoid looking at the horrific casualties, and unexplainable carnage.

They slowly rode Barney and Blue around the broken vehicles, the scattered trash and bodies, and then up to the barrier.

They sat on the horses, side by side, looking at the fence. The horses were obediently still, and keeping the damp girls heated with their radiantly warm bodies. It was quiet but for the pounding surf and the occasional cry of a shore bird hunting in the night. A piece of sheet metal pushed up against the fence on its side was clanking gently against the fence in the slight, foggy breeze. They both noticed it, but said nothing about it. The waves crashed hard on the sandy beach and rushed up to the shallows, spreading out foam, and sounding like an applause. As the waves rushed out, thousands of tiny sand fleas dislodged by the surge tried frantically to crawl back into the sand. Anne thought it looked like the ground was boiling. She looked back at the fence, breathed in deep and let out a slow breath. "Here we are."

Adela looked over at her with her smile of approval, and nodded silently, confirming Anne's deduction.

They sat and contemplated their next move.

The barrier was basically a fence. It was fifteen feet high, covered with cyclone fencing, topped with concertina razor wire, and running from far inland, out to the low tide line. If the tide was in, it was basically unpassable. But the tide was out by the time they had reached it.

Adela looked towards the surf line and could see that as the waves surged back out, they briefly left enough room to get around the last post of the fence, through a few feet of water. She turned Blue around, and he walked towards the end of the barrier, and closer to the intermittent path that was briefly exposed with each receding wave.

Anne watched her and knew she was going around. "Please don't, Adela! Please!" She felt as if she were watching her walk off the edge of something, where there was no return. "Adela! No!" she yelled.

But Adela followed the fence line, and as the wave rushed out, she dug her heels into Blue's flanks, and he lurched forward into the surf, splashing through knee deep water with a high stepping gait, and easily getting around the barrier. She rode him back up onto the beach, then just sat there on Blue, looking at Anne, through the barrier, from the forbidden side. "I won't ask you to follow any further, Anne. You can wait for me, or turn back."

"I can't go back alone, Adela." Anne was numb. "I'm lost right now. I can't make it by myself out here. You know I don't have a chance. Please, come back. I'm scared!"

Adela looked at Anne and smiled, turned Blue and walked south again. She did not look back.

Anne looked around at the mess on the beach. The bodies of people who were killed trying to get past this barrier, the trash, the burned-out trucks; the hell that she was now part of. *Where are the soldiers now?* She wondered. *Is it possible they stopped defending this area? Does it matter any more?*

Anne felt as if she were being called to her own execution. She solemnly turned Barney towards the ocean. As the surf rushed out, she took him and followed the surge to the end of the barrier. He splashed through the knee-deep water, rounded the last post, and then was practically pushed ashore by the latest set of incoming waves. Barney was soon kicking up sprays of sand, as he galloped through a forbidden place, to catch up to Blue.

She caught up to Adela and they rode side by side, not speaking. Adela had no more to say on the subject, and Anne was quiet because she was just afraid to speak, or make a sound.

They hadn't gone far, maybe a few hundred yards beyond the fence, when they were discovered.

Near Zero Tolerance

As they rode the dark and banned route, the absence of un-natural noise was broken by a faint thumping sound, that was gradually increasing in volume. It grew louder, then exponentially louder, and then near deafening as the helicopter arrived. It hovered above them, while shining a bright spotlight on their position. The horses began to nervously turn and jump at the dangerously loud noise, the sudden intrusion of bright white light, and the commanding presence of the frightening aircraft.

The rotor wash from the weaponized ship swirled masses of sand and loose beach debris into the air, and into their faces and eyes, as they did their best to control their terrified steeds.

Soon, several Humvees and military vehicles were on the scene, their spotlights harshly illuminating the women, the immediate area, and searching in all directions for any other trespassers who may be part of Adela's challenge to the responding security force, who had clearly posted warnings of the consequences of crossing the fence, and entering into this forbidden zone.

Adela fought her instinct to run. Because she knew that if she fled, that it would be her very last act of defiance.

A loudspeaker from the gunship announced, "You are in a restricted area! Do not move, or you will be fired upon!" Barney reared up, but Anne hung on. She tried to calm him, but he was not wanting to be still. She turned in his reins as he tried to bolt, causing him to step lively to the left, and spinning them around. Eventually, she had him correctly facing the soldiers.

The women were shocked at the rapid and overwhelming response. They held up their hands briefly, but had to quickly drop them to control the reins, to keep the horses from bolting. They needed to hold the reins low and close to keep Barney and Blue in position, and that was probably contrary to what was expected of a surrendering person.

The trucks moved in closer and Anne could see several soldiers climbing down from the vehicles, advancing on them with rifles pointed. They were now surrounded, and about to be dealt with.

The helicopter overhead relinquished control of the violators and horses to the ground forces, gained altitude, and then flew off to check the fence line for more possible intruders.

"Please don't shoot!" Anne cried.

The soldiers stood firm, waiting for the next command. A siren began to wail in the distance.

Everybody stood as still and quiet as possible, as diesel engines idled on. Soldiers' shadows could be seen behind the lights, creeping into position, as Anne and Adela awaited their fate. Radio traffic crackled from the truck that was in the center of the half circle formation of vehicles. They could faintly hear a man talking into a radio, getting information and issuing commands. Through the glaring wash of light, they could hear a truck door open. A soldier climbed out and began walking toward them.

He approached with two rifle bearing soldiers, one on each side of him. He looked up at the girls on the horses and said nothing. He spoke into his radio, with his eyes locked onto the riders in front of him. "Red team! Check the line. Check your perimeter. We have two subjects inside 'G' sector."

"Red Team. Blue Leader, copy," was the reply from the radio. "Two in sector 'G', checking the line."

Seven high intensity spotlights were on the women, completely blinding them, and lighting the scene with warm beams that constantly scanned and shifted shadows, as they searched for any other bold intruders who would be part of this peculiar incursion.

Anne looked at Adela and Blue, and saw them covered in little red dots that seemed to jump around as they moved, only to settle on their chests and faces. She suddenly realized that the little red laser dots were covering her as well. She held up her hand to shield her eyes from the offending glare.

"Get off the horses," the commander instructed. They climbed down from Barney and Blue, and stood on the beach, holding their reins.

"Check those horses and packs!" the officer ordered.

A sergeant standing in the immediate group spoke into his radio headset, and six soldiers moved up and took control of the search. One man held the reins and calmed the horse, while a second man checked and scanned the saddles and packs with several instruments, for any signs of radiation, metal, chemicals, explosives or weapons. The remaining two stood by to cover the women with deadly crossfire, if necessary.

They stood on the beach while their horses were being searched. They held their hands above their heads, looking forward, towards the voice that was instructing them.

"Who else is here with you two?" the officer demanded simply and loudly, in a tone that promised great consequences at any attempt of silence or diversion.

"Nobody! Just us!" Adela answered quickly.

"What are your intentions?" he asked angrily.

"I'm here to pray for the launches, sir!" Adela confessed.

The lieutenant wanted to believe the answer, but was not impressed with it. "I have orders to shoot on site any intruders inside this area. You, are inside this area!" His command on either side of him stepped forward, because he stepped forward. Their rifles pointed at the women's torsos. Two soldiers moved in and began to scan and search them for weapons.

The lieutenant stood staring at them, analyzing their behavior.

"We knew we shouldn't have come in, sir. We talked about it a lot; that it would be dangerous and we would be killed, but... I don't know, sir. It just happened." Anne had told the truth. And for the first time had even explained it to herself. And now, she felt kind of stupid, like she was coming out of a fog. She looked at Adela, and of course, Adela simply smiled back.

A soldier approached the sergeant, who was standing near the lieutenant, and made his report, "Sir, they're clean. Just some clothes and food. Looks like chicken."

"It's rabbit," Adela corrected.

"Were did you get it?" the lieutenant demanded.

"We caught it! In the mountains! Skinned it and cooked it on a small fire," Anne interjected proudly. "It's ours!" she added bluntly, but fast became sheepish, as the lieutenant stared back, not appreciating opinions or the slightest defiance of his command.

"Is that so?" he replied. "I don't want your stinky rabbit." He pushed the package into Anne's hands.

"It's not stinky," Anne protested quietly.

He continued his stare down with her, as he instructed his command to stand down, and they did, except for the two soldiers on either side of him. They held their rifles on the girls at all times, without pause.

With the lieutenant, there were no mistakes, and his command was tight. No advantage would be given on his watch. He knew they were young girls, and he knew they were innocent. But his command needed him. His safety would not be compromised under his strict protocol, unless he himself waded into dangerous point positions, which he was known to do.

"People will kill you for this, you know," he advised them sternly.

"For our food?" Adela looked at Anne and they both knew all about it, but did not tell.

"Yes." He wasn't sure if they were aware of the food distribution effort, so he told them,

"If you want food, you have to go to Bakersfield, that is the nearest food distribution point in this region, and I understand that even they are running out of supplies."

"Is that why there is so few people here on the coast? Is that why everybody left?" Anne wondered.

"That's right, ma'am." the lieutenant confirmed. "The souls who are tough enough to stick it out here are also dangerous people sometimes. They might kill you for those horses, ma'am."

"We call them meat hunters, sir. And yes, they are dangerous and desperate. They killed a pack horse that we couldn't bring with us, because she was too old," Anne complained.

"Meat hunters? That's what you call them? Hmm." The lieutenant liked the term. However, he realized that enough time had been spent with these two, and he needed to move on to other threats.

"Here's what you're going to do," he ordered. "You will ride out of here the same way that you came in. If you turn back, we will fire upon you." Anne was scared and she showed it. Adela was smiling back at him, admiring this brave man, who is part of humanity's last great struggle for survival.

He did his best to not smile back, and he didn't. But he did lean in to emphasize an important point. "That means you die; we kill you. Understand?"

"Yes," they said in unison. Anne grabbed Adela's arm and held her close for protection. She was scared of the soldiers, but more afraid to be released from the safety of their presence.

The lieutenant turned around and waved a soldier over to him. The soldier trotted over at a brisk pace. "Yes, sir!" he reported.

"Sargent, bring up an MRE."

"Sir!" he replied, and ran back to the line of trucks idling on the sand dunes.

"Do you think we could get some water for our horses? We have at least an eight-mile ride back before they can drink again, Please, sir?" Anne pleaded to the lieutenant.

Adela turned and looked at Anne. "Good thinking!"

The lieutenant sighed at the request. The sergeant ran up with the MRE package and handed it to the lieutenant. He took the ration, then ordered, "Sargent, bring up two gallons of fresh water."

"Sir!" the sergeant acknowledged, turned around, and again ran back towards the line of trucks to fulfill the order.

The sergeant went to the back of his Humvee, and opened the rear door. Two soldiers were standing by in their stand down positions, but definitely still watching the lieutenant. A private walked up to the sergeant. "Are those girls friendly?

The sergeant pulled out a two and half gallon plastic container of water and closed the rear door. "Yeah, they're friendly, but I think he may have gone sweet on them."

The private was a bit shocked at that observation, "Really? The lieutenant?" He shook his head in pretend confusion and let out a chuckle.

The sergeant again ran back to the lieutenant with his water. "Sir! Two and a half gallons!"

The lieutenant pointed to the ground, and the sergeant set the water at Adela's feet. He then handed her the MRE pouch. "I want you to take this. I know you can find your own food, rabbits and what not, but take it anyway."

"Thank you, sir. It's very much appreciated," Adela said sincerely.

"Yes, thank you, sir," Anne agreed, without knowing what he was handing her.

The lieutenant looked over Anne's shoulder and waved in the soldiers who had been in charge of the horses. The soldiers walked Blue and Barney over to the lieutenant. The lieutenant pointed at the women, and the soldiers knew he was ordering them to hand the horses back to the girls.

"Do whatever you have to do to get them watered, you have five minutes." He stood there and watched them go to work.

Adela went to Blue's saddle bag and produced a foldable canvas bucket. She opened it up and began filling it with water. Barney also had a foldable bucket in his saddle bag, and Anne brought that out to be filled as well. The horses dipped their muzzles into the buckets and drank.

Adela filled her canteen, and Anne put her water bottle out to be filled too.

The lieutenant watched the horses drink. "What are their names?" he asked uncharacteristically.

Adela was kneeling in the sand next to Blue. She looked up at the lieutenant and met his smile. "This is Blue…"

"And this is Barney," Anne added to Adela's answer.

The lieutenant folded his arms, in a more relaxed but stoic gesture and said, "My girl had a pony she called Raven." He looked down, recollecting distant memories. "He was black as coal." His mind began wandering to places far away. "She loved that horse," he remembered fondly. Adela glanced at Anne and they caught each other's smile.

He cleared his throat, regained his composure, and soon ordered, "Okay, girls! That's it! Mount up and move on!"

The girls took away the buckets, emptied the little remaining water into the sand, then replaced the buckets in the saddle bags and were about to saddle up, when the ground began to rumble.

The entire platoon of soldiers and the girls watched the horizon begin to glow. The rumbling grew louder. Adela knew they were launching a rocket. The launch pad was less than a mile away, so the roar was very intimate now. She could feel the pressure waves from the mighty rocket thrusting against the Earth, pushing its multi-ton payload off the ground and beyond the gravitational pull of her planet. The horses began to get excited again, and began to kick and jump. The women held their reins, and did not let them escape their control. The rocket climbed far into the sky, and released its first stage, which flew off to the side and began its descent back to Earth. The rocket's secondary engines began thrusting, and it continued its laborious climb.

Adela fell to her knees, trying to hold Blue's reins while she put her palms together and held them to her chest, looking like a little schoolgirl in church who had come to pray. She began loudly enough to be heard over the roar of the explosive engines, overhead:

"Our Father who art in Heaven, hallowed be Thy name, Thy kingdom come, Thy will be done on Earth as it is in Heaven. Give us this day, our daily bread, and forgive us our trespasses, as we forgive those who trespass against us. And lead us not into temptation, but deliver us from evil."

"Amen," the lieutenant said.

Adela looked up at him, and noticed he had his cap off. She closed her eyes and continued, loudly, over the angry rumble of the atmosphere.

"Please, God, reveal yourself! In our most desperate hour! Who are you?" she cried. "God, Jesus, Krishna, Apollo, whatever your name! Whatever your power! Please! Help us find the wisdom to preserve our humble planet. We are fighting now! Please, join our struggle! Now! You must guide us in our most desperate hour. You must not leave us alone in this fight. Now is the time to deliver us from evil. Dear Lord, bring yourself close, and let these good rockets find their sacred targets! Amen."

Adela opened her eyes, looked around, and could tell all the soldiers within earshot had heard her. Most had followed her unorthodox prayer. Many had their hats off. She could hear the refrain of 'Amen' coming from different soldiers at different moments. All the soldiers put their caps back on their heads, and resumed watching the girls and horses.

The rocket launch was successful so far, and the ship had disappeared into space. The lieutenant leaned over, grabbed Adela's arm and pulled her to her feet from her prayer position. "C'mon, girl. That's a beautiful prayer, but you need to saddle up, and leave here. Now!" He started pushing her closer towards Blue's stirrup. She allowed the shove, and went along with it.

She grabbed the saddle horn, put her foot up high in the stirrup, and pulled herself up onto Blue's back. She sat up straight and high, and looked down to ask the lieutenant, "We saw explosions in space earlier tonight, on our way here. Were they nukes? Did they hit our target?" She was hopeful.

The lieutenant looked up and could see her brown eyes locked onto his. He knew she was worthy of the truth. There was nothing wrong with her in his opinion. Her actions, although extremely dangerous to her and her friend, were not completely unreasonable in this final fight. He had an attraction for this type of personality, and he knew that in the civilized world as he knew it, she would be a good, and loyal friend. "We don't know, yet." He half-smiled at her briefly, then turned away and walked back towards his truck.

He must know something! Adela thought to herself. *Why else would he be working so hard to protect this area? How does he keep his men from running off? Yea*, she thought, *he knows something!* She smiled to herself, and watched him walk away.

"Lieutenant!" she cried after him.

He stopped and turned to look at her. He had just about had it with this one. "What?" he barked back, in an angry and final tone.

"You're a good man. A good human being!" she cried out loudly enough to be heard by many, then leaned forward and bumped Blue with her heels. He began an easy trot, with Anne and Barney following, back towards the fence that had almost kept them out.

The commander, satisfied they were on their way, climbed back into his truck, and the convoy began to pull away and follow the horses down the beach.

When they reached the fence, the trucks aimed their spotlights at the end of the of barrier, to guide the way around the last post in the surf line. The waves surged out, and the girls and horses splashed around the end of the last post. The water was a little deeper now because the tide was turning, and now coming in, but the horses pushed through the chest deep water, and then lunged back up onto the beach, to the dry sand. They stood on the other side, dripping streams of water and facing the platoon from the safe side of the fence. They waved at the line of Humvees that were still lighting them, then turned together and rode off. The soldiers watched them bounce away, on their wet galloping horses.

The lieutenant was worried about them. He wanted them to have every advantage. He watched them negotiate the random and unfortunate combat debris that littered the beach. When he was satisfied that they had cleared most of the larger obstacles, he spoke into his radio. "Kill the lights!"

The spotlights went out, quickly faded, and the riders disappeared into the darkness. That was the best he could do for them.

The tide was coming up and the waves were getting bigger and louder. The lieutenant thought about Adela's prayer and her last question to him. He turned to his driver. "Move out, Corporal!" He ordered. The convoy pulled away and drove off to find other threats.

Apology

The horses slowed from their gallop and returned to a relaxed, ambling gait. They were settling in for the long ride back, so they let the horses, more or less, find their own comfortable pace and position. Anne observed how Blue naturally led, and Barney naturally followed. They continued north, mostly in this single file formation, with Anne letting Barney lag behind for the first few miles.

She kicked Barney and he went into a trot. She wanted to get close enough to Adela to speak to her in a normal tone, above the waves and occasional light gust of wind. Adela noticed that she was trying to catch up, so she pulled up on Blue's reins. Barney thumped up to Blue in three-quarter time. "Whoa!" Anne commanded Barney, as he approached them. She didn't really need to pull up on his reins. He knew what she wanted, and he delivered them right to the side of Blue. Blue tossed his head slightly and offered a snort and a nicker in greeting.

"And that's *why* we shouldn't go past the fence," Anne critique latently, sarcastically and decisively.

Adela thought that was funny, so she laughed, "Ha! Good one!" She turned to look at Anne's face, "I think it made a difference."

Barney began to slow a bit, so Anne flicked his reins and he moved up closer, alongside Blue. Her reward of neck scratching and encouraging words appealed to his horse reason, and sent him the message that this is where he is supposed to be. So, he began to keep pace, side by side with Blue, without much more effort from Anne.

She then replied, "Oh really? Wouldn't it have been a little less dangerous. And less scary as hell, by the way, to just do the praying thing on the safe side of that fence?"

Adela put her finger to her chin, pretending to ponder the question. After a few moments of the pantomime, she said decidedly, "No. I don't think so." She looked at the sky and could tell it would be daylight in a few hours, then amended the answer to Anne's question. "Also, I didn't like all the bodies and wrecks. Bad vibes."

"Bad vibes?" Anne was unsatisfied with Adela's simple reply. She didn't really want to be around dead bodies either, so that was a given. But it wasn't really a legitimate excuse to jump the fence. "I don't understand how it made a difference on the dangerous side of that fence, as opposed to the safer side." She was still not buying into Adela's 'mission'.

She finally said exactly what she was thinking. "I think you're reckless sometimes; you scare me sometimes." Then she added, "No, you scare me often." She giggled nervously at Adela's risky behavior, "Basically, you do scary shit constantly."

"You don't think our mission was successful? Not worth it?"

"Sure, I guess it was if you believe it was. But that's not what I mean, and you know it. Your prayers are fine, but it's where you insist praying that's getting us into dangerous situations." She finally added, "You can't use simple words as a shield, if you continue to intentionally put yourself in dangerous places."

Adela pulled up on Blue and looked downwards, contemplating the statement. She looked at Anne with calm eyes. "Why not?"

"If there is a God, I don't think he listens," Anne admitted.

"Well, if you're going to be heard, it has to come from a place of sincerity."

"Yeah, I get it by now, but that's beyond sincere, that's just plain old reckless abandon."

"Yeah, I know. Like I said: sincere."

"God is supposedly out there somewhere and we're down here, so it's not like we can even hear each other, or that a few hundred feet could even make a difference."

"That's your opinion, Anne. But consider the power of positive thoughts, regardless of who we pray to. I don't expect God to actually do anything, either. I pray for wisdom, mostly. I think the answers are already here with us. If there really is a creator, then it must have made us with the power of discovery. Maybe it left us with the power to control our own fate as well." She patted Blue on the neck and he lifted his head slightly and put his ears forward, in response to the kind gesture.

"If the answers are all here, then how do we find them?" Anne said, trying to stay logical.

"Pray for wisdom." Then she added, "You see, Anne, life is like a treasure hunt. The things you need to perform your most desperate act are here already, they just haven't been recognized or understood yet." They rode along while Anne was trying to understand. Adela added, "We weren't designed to fail; that's our niche. It's our purpose as a species to learn and succeed as a species through knowledge. That's all we can do. In many ways, it makes us horrible and dastardly. But in some ways, our design makes us the only hope for all living things. Especially on a day like today." She had a deep sigh, and then reached way over to put her hand on Anne's shoulder. "So fucking ironic! Isn't it?"

Anne wasn't angry any more, she just wanted to know how Adela worked. She was beginning to understand her position, and realized that it wasn't really weird or unspiritual, but actually kind of refreshing and thoughtful. "So, who were you praying to?"

"My prayers were just positive energy that I was sending along with the rockets."

"So, you were praying to the rocket?" She gave up trying to predict answers.

"Sort of."

The horses plodded along. The waves running up on the beach were not rushing out as fast as they were earlier. The tide was coming in. Sand pipers peeped staccato cries and long wails in the dark. Anne shrugged her shoulders, realizing she had it all wrong about Adela's religious convictions.

"That's weird. I thought you were praying to God," she admitted.

"You don't think that those rockets have the power to determine the fate of humanity, and all life on our planet?"

Anne caught the relative idea. "Interesting." She stood in her stirrups, easing her slightly sore rear end.

"If God is everything, then God is also a rocket," Adela believed. "A true destroyer, or savior of humanity. Literally." She looked at Anne and raised her eyebrow, as if the conundrum had been solved.

Anne laughed. "I bet those soldiers didn't know that they were praying to a rocket!"

Adela countered, "It doesn't matter who, or what God is. If God is real, then God can hear. If God can't hear, then real or not, God is pretty damn useless."

"Yeah, that makes sense," Anne agreed quickly.

Adela continued. "Oh, they were praying to their God, all right. Some probably just praying. But if they were praying to their God, to assist the man-made rocket, then yeah, that's kind of like praying to a rocket. I can see how that seems weird. But I don't care, it's all we got left; we're out of options. And if we hadn't gone beyond that barrier, none of them would have prayed with me. We rallied a lot of energy tonight, Anne." Adela had a big smile on her face. "We did what we came to do in our fight for humanity and our home. We were very successful. I feel really good about it. And hopeful!" She looked over at the orangish quarter moon setting into the Pacific Ocean.

"Well, I think praying to a rocket seems kind of cultish," Anne said decisively.

Adela giggled at the idea. "It would be a cult, if I had followers. But I'm just sending my energy to whatever God would even care." She thought more about it. "No religious denomination has the right to, or control over, spiritual events or efforts, they just think they do. You don't have to be Christian, or Catholic, or Protestant, or Jewish, or Hindu, or whatever, to experience miracles. And we may have the power to send energy out to the universe, and maybe even direct it. I mean, we are energy, right? We are composed of vibrations. And we are bombarded with energy constantly, from all points of our universe. It is received, and sent. I believe we sent a very sincere, clear message tonight, and I'm glad we did it."

The horses walked side by side, each in two-four time, but out of time with each other, their hoofs scrunching into the softness of the beach, throwing up spoonsful of sand with each lifted hoof, as they clomped along.

"Anyhoo, it sure beats sitting in the cave waiting for the world come to an end." She looked over at Anne and smiled a big smile.

Anne smiled back. She thought about the beautiful oasis at the wave and wondered if she would be less miserable there.

Adela certainly had them busy and occupied. Her mission had definitely, on many occasions, distracted Anne from the impending doom that was constantly lurking overhead.

"Yeah, I guess it does. In a way," she agreed tentatively. "We're still managing ways to stay alive and vital, I guess." She changed the subject. "Hey, why didn't the soldiers find the ranger's gun?"

"I ditched it in the canyon where we last camped. It's behind that rock that you liked to sit on."

"Dang, Adela!" Anne was stunned. "I thought we had a gun with us! I sort of felt better with that protection. What if we need it again?" She was suddenly feeling frightfully vulnerable. Especially since they still had to get past the town, and sneak back under the freeway.

'I don't want to kill anybody, any more. One was too much, Anne. I'll never touch another God-damned gun again! Never."

"Well, shit. I would have carried it!" Anne was angry that she wasn't told about it being left in the canyon. However, she admitted, "It's probably best we didn't have it when we were searched."

"You're welcome!" Adela shot back with a sing-song melody in her voice.

"Whatever." Anne knew she was right.

She wasn't really mad at Adela for leaving the weapon behind, she was just a little bit defeated at the realization of the fact that Adela's ditching of the gun, no matter how tragic it seemed at the present moment, had actually, probably, worked out for the best. The soldiers may not have been very understanding, and would likely had confiscated it, or found it to be a hostile threat. Its discovery could have caused a completely different outcome.

"Is there anything else that you have done, that you haven't told me about?"

Adela put her hand to chin to again, sarcastically pantomiming extreme thought again. "Hmmm. Nope!" She looked ahead, not caring what Anne thought about her ditching the pistol. Anne felt a bit disregarded that she hadn't been consulted about it in the first place. But she knew it must be forgiven, and forgotten. There is still dangerous ground to cover, and although Adela really was hard to understand, and appeared foolhardy at times, she really was glad to be with her.

MRE

"What's in that package the lieutenant gave you?" Anne suddenly remembered.

"Oh yeah! I almost forgot!" Adela pulled back on Blue's reins and he stopped.

Barney stopped even before Anne pulled up on his reins, and he stood there next to Blue. Anne pulled the reins slightly to the right, and tapped his flank with her heel, and he leaned into Blue. She could feel the weight of both horses squeezing her leg between them, trapping it tightly, in a warm and comfortable horse flesh vice. They stayed very close to each other while Adela reached around to find the MRE that the lieutenant had given them. "Here it is." She held the package in the moonlight and studied it.

The package was about the size of a loaf of bread. It was thick plastic and military desert brown in color, with black lettering that read: MRE. MRE is the designated acronym for Meals Ready to Eat, a military meal designed to be eaten in the field, on the go. Adela pulled it open like a person pulls open a bag of potato chips. Inside she found multiple smaller bags, each little package containing an element of the multi course, shelf stable meal. She began pulling out individual package's and handing them over to Anne.

"Pepperoni pizza slice... Oatmeal cookie!... Cherry blueberry cobbler... Italian bread sticks!" They were stunned at all these comfort foods in a military ration.

"Open that pizza!" Adela ordered. Anne pulled the package open and pulled out the pizza slice. She put it to her mouth and took a big bite, then handed it to Adela. Adela took a bite and closed her eyes as she savored the spices, cheese, pepperoni and sauce. Flavors that she had almost forgotten about. "Oh, my Gawd!" She was in a kind of flavor ecstasy. She spoke with her mouth full, muffling her words. "Dis is da bes peeta eh-er." She chewed well and swallowed, had another big bite, then handed it back to Anne.

Anne finished it in two bites, then opened the breadsticks. They tasted more like a flatbread, but they didn't complain. They were very flavorful and they could taste the well-preserved flavors of basil, thyme, salt, pepper and garlic. They chewed them up happily while Anne opened the oatmeal cookie. Adela opened the accessory packages and found matches, salt, pepper and sugar packs, a small ration of toilet paper, a wet towelette pack, plastic spoon in its own cellophane package, creamer, gum and coffee instant type II. "No way," she said laughingly.

"What?" Anne anticipated.

"Instant coffee!" Adela smiled at Anne like the best thing in the world had just happened.

"Ni-i-ice!" Anne agreed.

Adela brought up her water bottle and held it between her legs while she opened the coffee pouch. She poured it into her remaining water, closed the cap and shook vigorously. She didn't bother putting in creamer or sugar. "Give it a minute to dissolve." She pulled out another package. "Chocolate protein drink powder!" She handed it Anne. "Pour it in your water bottle and shake it up!" Anne took the package and brought up her water bottle, placing it between her legs. She opened the little package and dumped the mixture in. She closed the top and shook it up well.

Adela shook her bottle once more, opened the lid and had her first drink of coffee in many months. "Oh yeah, that is the best coffee ever!" She handed the delicious draft to Anne.

Anne took big swig and confirmed, "Yes, It's so good! God, I miss coffee!" She wiped her mouth with the back of her hand. "What's up with that cobbler?" she said, smiling widely at Adela.

Adela brought it up and gave it a squeeze. "Feels kind of mushy, I'm not sure how to eat it." She decided to tear off the corner of the bag with her teeth and squeeze it out like a pastry bag. She leaned her head back slightly, and squeezed out a glob towards her open mouth. Most of it made it into her mouth, but some fell onto her shirt, and a little ran down her chin.

"Give me some of that!" Anne demanded playfully demanded. Adela handed it over and Anne squeezed out a big mouthful of the sweet and sticky ration, also spilling some of the juice down her chin. They finished off the bag of cobbler, drank the coffee, then used the wet towelette to wipe their sticky hands and faces. "Anything else in there?" Anne asked in her most curious tone.

Adela rummaged through the bag and inspected the balance. "Let's see. Cheese spread with jalapeno, aw, man… we could have put that on the breadsticks, oh well. Toilet paper!"

"Wow!" Anne was elated. "I want some!"

"Cheese spread, or toilet paper?" Adela giggled.

"Like you don't know! Ha-ha." They laughed at the comedy of having to make the choice.

Adela regained her composure and continued, "Flameless ration heater. We can save that for something else, I guess. Spoon, matches. Nice, gum!"

"Gimme a piece," Anne begged. Adela squeezed the gum package and two pieces of candy covered gum popped out into her hand. She handed a piece to Anne. Anne popped it in her mouth and began chewing. "Thank you, Lieutenant!" she said out loud.

"He was an awesome guy," Adela declared.

"Yeah, he was!" Anne agreed. "If I ever see him again, I'm gonna give him a big kiss!"

"Screw that!" Adela countered. "I'll suck his dick!" The girls began laughing hysterically at the idea.

"Why you nasty, little slut!" Anne said accusingly, and shook her head in mock disappointment at Adela's shocking and hilarious reply.

"Well, we are talking about pizza and coffee," Adela chuckled.

"He said he would 'kill us' if he saw us again!" Anne reminded her laughingly.

"Mmm …So hot! Kill me, Lieutenant!" Adela's comically sadistic reply had them laughing again, forgetting about the world and its miserable condition, and unwittingly celebrating their situation, with loud voices.

"He was good looking!" Anne remembered.

"Yeah, he was totally a catch. I bet he likes football," Adela guessed.

"Naw!" Anne countered. "He's into making me breakfast in bed, and taking me sailing!" She looked at Adela sideways, expecting a smart-aleck reply.

"Oh, bullshit! I saw him first!" They chuckled together, and then became quiet in thought.

Adela remembered that the day was approaching. The smile left her face as she studied the horizon and night sky. They had to move on if they were going to use the darkness and early hours as cover to sneak around the town that was their last obstacle, before getting back into the safety of the forest.

"Let's get moving." She gently kicked Blue in the flanks with her heels, and he began walking forward. Barney immediately began following, as they continued down the beach, towards the creek that led to the tunnel. They didn't say any more about the lieutenant, but rode through the damp and misty darkness without speaking, for the next few miles.

A Trap

Soon they could see the developing shadows and shapes of the buildings and houses of the abandoned town, in the pre-dawn hour. They were close to their last obstacle. Adela had hoped that traveling in the early morning hours would give her an advantage, and that was true, but she also knew that hungry people don't sleep very well.

Blue's ears began twitching, and he let out a snort. His head was up, and he became anxious. Barney sensed it too, and started to nervously side step. Anne corrected him and tried to calm him. "Easy, boy," she cooed, stroking his neck, trying to reassure him, while looking around in all directions for whatever was making the horses nervous.

They stopped and stood still to listen. Anne was unable to see any threat. The surf pounded and its waves washed up towards the high tide line. The horses stepped up as the rushing water swirled around their legs. "What's wrong?" she whispered.

"The horses see or sense something." Adela's experience with horses reminded her that they have excellent vision, smell and hearing. She twisted herself in the saddle to look behind them, and could see nothing but darkness. Then she noticed a faint glow on the beach up ahead. "There's a fire on the beach, Anne," she pointed out.

Now Anne could barely see the glow too. "Is that what they're nervous about?"

"Hmm …No, I don't think so." Adela knew it was not the source of their equine concern. "Well, shoot! We can't go that way, Anne." Adela knew the beach access into town would be possible to negotiate, but if they try to go through, it could be the end of Blue and Barney. She again looked down the beach at the distant and flickering bonfire that was blocking their route. She took her binoculars from her pack and looked. She thought she could see several people around the fire, and some of them might have what look like rifles. But it was so dark and far away, that she couldn't be certain.

She leaned forward in her saddle and looked over at Anne. "I think they're waiting for us," she said calmly.

Adrenaline coursed through Anne's body and she fought the panic. "Damn! Did they see us come through this morning?"

"Probably," Adela concurred. She knew they were about to be trapped, so it was critical to make their move now. She knew it didn't have to be a confrontation; they could make it easy. She looked through the binoculars again, and spoke as she watched the enemy. "We can let them have the horses and escape on foot, or we can fight for them."

"Give them Barney and Blue?" Anne was extremely distraught at the very idea. "I don't want to give them up, Adela! I won't let them be destroyed by those vile trolls!" Her eyes were welling up, and her anger was rising. She squinted through tears at the distant fire speck down the beach. "I want to keep Barney!" she blurted out, surprising herself. "I mean, we can go the other way, right?"

Adela smiled at Anne. "I think were trapped, Anne. They know we're here." She did not like the odds.

The town was small, and was laid out along the coast. Its main street paralleled the surf line, while the freeway that connected it to the rest of the region ran between it and the coastal range foothills. Trying to cross over the freeway meant having to go through town, which was dangerous for the horses. The only safe way back was to go under the freeway. They needed to cross at the creek, or ride through miles of debris littered roads, replete with meat hunters and starving people.

If they tried to go through this mob on the beach, there was a good chance they would lose the horses, and likely get killed themselves. Turning around offers no safety either. The military is watching for them and will shoot to kill. So, that's definitely not helpful. They could try to go through the dunes, but they would still eventually need to cross the freeway, to get back to the safety of the coastal range.

Anne was watching Adela think about it. She could see her studying the situation, and didn't expect her to shy away from any extreme measure. She spoke up. "They won't make it through town, Adela. Don't even suggest it!" She looked down the beach at the speck of light. "We have to go back!"

"Go back?" She looked at Anne like she just wasn't getting it. "There is no 'back', Anne."

"Let's go into the dunes, then," Anne reasoned.

"We could, but we still have to get over the freeway!" Adela countered. She looked out over the dunes and thought maybe it would be best to go into them. She looked back at the trail leading up to the town. She looked at the beach gang, and noticed their fire was growing.

Together they sat, quietly rethinking the dilemma and contemplating their escape or surrender.

"Well, if we do need to go through town, we could get onto the main street that way." Adela pointed to a trail that led from the beach, up to a cul-de-sac, at the very south end of the beach town. Anne could see the white sand trail that was splitting through the ice plant and leading up to the neighborhood.

Adela, with a stiff upper lip, knew they had to move now. She did not like the idea of having to go through the dunes, then into larger residential neighborhoods, in order to reach the freeway, and then have find their way across. The foothills were just at the end of this beach and if that group of predators weren't blocking it, they would be on their way back to the safety of the mountains. "I guess we have no choice; through the dunes it is."

She turned Blue and began walking south again. Anne gently nudged Barney's flanks and he quickly moved up towards Blue. Adela thought she could see a trail leading into the gentle sand dunes.

Blue snorted and twitched his ears. Adela understood his warning, and pulled him to a stop to listen. The silence of the early morning was broken by a spinning starter and ignition of a diesel motor.

Bright flood lights suddenly blinded the women and horses, as the truck pulled out from behind a dune and revved towards them. Blue immediately turned away from the offense, and Adela did not try to stop him, but kicked his flanks, switched his thigh, and yelled out as loud as she could, "Hee-Yaa!" the command that any horse knows means, 'Go. Now. Fast.' Blue bolted with a pulsing gait that accelerated with each galloping lunge, through the deep sand. Barney was right behind, kicking sand with all his might. The herd was in full escape mode.

The pickup truck, badly driven, wasted momentum and speed by racing its engine at slow speeds, and then going into wide fishtail corrections as it's tires spun and tried to find traction in the deep

213

sand. The driver clearly had trouble handling the truck, as they tried to wrangle the fleeing prey. It was using precious fuel to drive these horses into a trap, and if this fails, then the ranger's stolen truck will soon just sputter out and quit, to become yet another useless, immovable, technological mess.

The gang waiting at the end of the beach could see the floodlit running horses. They stood around their fire waiting for the game to come to them. They knew all about those horses. They had already eaten the grey that Adela had let out, but they knew that there were others. They had discovered the ranger's cabin. They knew there were two more horses with riders on this beach. And they were going to take them.

The last of the livestock were gone now. Cattle, sheep and pigs were rare. Horses were considered food. These towns were abandoned because of lack of food. So, these horses were absolutely wanted by the meat hunters.

Game species like deer were driven back, and extremely wary and difficult to hunt due to the clumsy over hunting and random methods used by the meat hunters and other desperate survivors. Their poor marksmanship and careless mobs teach the game species that being near man is a fatal trap. So, they quickly lose trust, and increase their distance away from the things of man, and decrease their tolerance of man. There is nothing to gain from being near man any more.

The meat hunters watched the lights from the chase truck going in the wrong direction.

The pale green truck tried to herd them towards the fire on the beach, but its bad driver did not anticipate them going into the hopelessly clogged town streets.

The Hungry Gauntlet

Adela led her charging group up the trail, towards the cul-de-sac. Anne was right behind.

They didn't want to go through the town, but now they had no choice. The truck could have easily chased them into the dunes and ran them down, if they hadn't decided to escape into town, a move that was not expected by the meat hunters.

The full-sized pick-up could not follow the path into the cul-de-sac. This cul-de-sac barrier easily blocked traffic from the beach side. The truck turned around, throwing a rooster tail of sand in a semi-circle, then raced north, across the beach, looking for another beach access into the ruined municipality.

The horses cantered through the backstreets and the deserted neighborhood in three-quarter time, their hoofs clomping like coconut cups on the hard pavement. They continually had to slow down and walk around broken cars, sofas, shopping carts, and other useless items that had been scattered by the fleeing and ravaging masses.

Blue cut his foot on an old bent dryer, but was so full of adrenaline, that he didn't notice the laceration, or the blood flowing down his hoof, that left a bloody hoofprint on his path. But so far, they were able to get through. If they can stay on this road to the dead end, they will have circumvented the beach gang, and hopefully get back onto the beach near the overpass tunnel. It wasn't far now!

Suddenly the green truck emerged from between two beach houses, revved the engine as it struggled through a side yard, throwing sand up that splattered the stucco walls of the deserted retreats, demonstrating the same bad driving skills, and immediately getting stuck between a jumble of dead automobiles. It was a dumb move by the truck's driver, and a lucky mistake for the girls. The horses broke into a run and galloped past them, as the hunters struggled to get out of their wreck with their rifles.

The girls knew that if the horses could make it to the end of the street, they could take the narrow access trail down the sandy hill, to the beach. The horses began to canter again through the increasingly obscured path, accidentally kicking and deflecting random objects, and causing the horses to short step, and nearly fall at times.

The beach gang tried to ambush them. They must have rushed up the coastal stairs to head them off. But they weren't fast enough. The horses galloped past them, just as they had passed the green truck, at a furious gait.

The crowd began shouting at them to stop, but they just rode on as fast as they could, ignoring any orders from the meat hunters. A shot was fired at the escaping women, hitting the rear-view mirror of a wrong-way-facing abandoned police car. Anne flinched at the sound of the impact, as the flying plastic and glass chips were blown in her direction.

Suddenly, Adela heard a slapping sound, then the rifle report reverberating up and down the street. Blue slowed down, began to limp, then began bucking, spinning, and whinnying in pain. He leaned hard to his left and then fell to the ground, throwing Adela against the side of a small sedan. She rolled over into the debris filled street to find Blue laying on his side. He was breathing, but not moving.

She quickly got up and limped after Barney and Anne. Anne pulled up on Barney's reins, and he skidded across the pavement, pushing debris with his pointed and sharp hoofs, then coming to a stop. He instinctively spun around, and with little prompting, leapt into a full speed gallop towards Adela. This horse was in the barrel race of his life.

Adela watched them come up fast, so she climbed up on a car hood. Barney began his stop before reaching Adela, and slid across the pavement, before bumping into the car that Adela was standing on. She jumped out, and landed gracefully, and luckily, on the horse's croup. Straddling his rump, she reached for Anne's waist and pulled herself up tight, over his hips. She kicked his flanks and he began to run, and run hard.

Barney knew this race, and he loved it. But he had never played it like this before. Somehow, he knew that this was about living or dying. He saw Blue in the street, and his adrenaline shot up. He would not lose this strange and frightful contest.

He raced through the car graveyard as fast as possible, with two girls and a saddle. He did his best to maintain a fast gallop. Often, he would have to slow to a canter, glancing off stalled vehicles, and jumping over little things, but Barney was very surefooted and tough. And when he came to a car blocking the sidewalk, nobody seemed particularly surprised when he jumped over, and cleared it, with a very secure and practiced landing. It was clear to Anne and Adela that Barney had much training in his past, and he loved to work. And right now, those skills were saving them.

They finally reached the street's end, and its embankment trail that led down to the beach. It was Anne's intention to find the path that led around the city road barrier at the dead end, before they had actually reached it. But perhaps due to miscommunication, or a misunderstanding, or because he was moving at a full gallop, Barney — who was secretly committed to going over the rail — simply ignored his rider. He intuitively launched the group from the edge of the pavement, clearing the four-foot barrier, and landing on a down slope that caused him to tumble, and throw them all down a sandy embankment that was covered in soft, thick ice plant. Barney rolled twice, but got up startled, but seemingly unfazed. He walked in a small circle, wondering what was next. The women, realizing they were unhurt, got up and cautiously approached Barney, hoping he wasn't harmed, or going to bolt away.

He didn't bolt, but stood by anxious, snorting, and waiting for his riders.

Adela, carefully reached for his reins. "Barney…Good boy!" Anne jumped up first, then helped Adela pull up behind her. They both sat tight on his back, as he again lunged into another full gallop, towards the tunnel.

"Ha!" Adela announced loudly. "We're back on the beach!"

"Ha!" Anne yelled as loud as she could. "Assholes!" she screamed, kicking Barney and holding up her middle finger to whoever could see it. The girls weren't laughing, but doing their best to antagonize their pursuers, in protest, while running for their lives. They knew that they were getting away. They were gaining distance and nothing could be done about it, as they galloped further on down the beach.

"Losers!" Anne shrieked, her voice breaking into a shrill scream.

"Re-tards!" Adela bellowed out as loud as she could. This caused the girls to actually laugh. They were ecstatic in their escape, and feeling freed, and victorious.

"Ya! Barney, ya!" Anne commanded as Barney pulsed faster and faster with each lunge of his accelerating gallop.

"Ya! Ya! Ya!" Adela cried, kicking at his flanks and slapping his rump as hard as she could.

A Fall

Barney moved down the surf line like a locomotive, alongside the pounding waves of the rising tide. A flash in the sky caught their periphery, and the girls looked up to see many nuclear explosions detonating far out in space, in a valiant effort to win the final fight.

Adela knew that her rocket was part of this volley of missiles. She cheered on the missiles, as they went to work trying to repel the global killer. Both girls were kicking Barney, as he raged on in his fury. "Ya! Ya!" Anne yelled as loud as she could, hoping everybody could hear.

"It's working, Anne! I think it's gonna work! *Yeee-haaw!*" Adela kicked Barney some more, and he put his head down and moved faster.

The sky lit up with a dozen tiny suns, back-lighting cloud formations, and causing electromagnetic disturbances that gave a very slight Aurora Borealis type light show, which illuminated the beach, the dead town and the nearby mountain range. The atmosphere began to lightly crackle and rumble.

Barney, kicking sand, wide eyed and whinnying, shook his head and ran even harder. He began to get mean.

Adela felt a hard slap on her back, like somebody hitting her hard with a club, followed by the report of a rifle shot, that echoed beyond them and back up the beach. Anne felt the hit too, but was padded and protected by her partner.

"I think I've been shot! Oh, I've been shot!" She leaned into Anne and put her face into her back. She lifted her head and coughed. Anne could feel a hot wet liquid spray onto her neck and the side of her face.

"Hang on, Adela! Don't let go!" she demanded. She could see the lagoon crossing approaching fast, and rode Barney into it at a full gallop.

He crashed into the chest deep water, causing a massive splash, and a wake that pushed a wall of water across the creek and up onto its banks.

The sudden stop was almost too much for Adela. Her grip loosened up in the impact. She was trying to stay focused, but her sudden and sustained loss of blood had her distracted, and unable to address more than one issue at a time. "He's a good horse, huh?" She spoke into Anne's ear, doing her best to hang on.

Anne was trying to hold onto her arm and hold the saddle horn at the same time; she could feel her letting go. "What?" Why would she want to talk about Barney at a time like this, she thought. "Don't let go!" she shouted at Adela over the splashing water, and the huffing and snorting horse, struggling to pull them across the pond.

"Barney! He's a good horse, huh?" It was a simple question, but it seemed like the middle of an endless conversation to Adela. She was losing her motor functions, and her brain was shutting down as her heart had no more blood to pump.

"He's a great horse!" Anne agreed in sympathy to Adela in her state of shock, and confusion. "Don't let go!" she demanded, through sandy tears.

Barney was in the deep water now and swimming with full angry strokes. His head dipped below the water, then popped back up, and this slowed them down as he struggled with his heavy riders. Anne knew they were pulling him under, so she let them float off his back. As Barney found shallow water, and his hoofs started to find traction, Anne pulled herself back onto the saddle while he was still submerged, but Adela could not. She at last became unconscious from her injuries, let go of her weak grip on Anne, and fell backwards, and into the dark water.

"Adela!" Anne screamed, trying to turn the fleeing horse in the chest deep water. She wanted to stop, and gather up Adela, but she knew she was gone; She watched her lifeless form slip beneath the water. She paused at the sudden and horrific loss, not knowing exactly what to do. She hesitated, and stalled, torn, wondering if there was a chance, a way, to see Adela one last time.

A bullet whistled past her head, sounding like a demonic hornet, followed by the crack of the rifle. Death was closing in on her. Anne had to go now.

Adela was lost.

She looked in the direction of her pursuers and screamed at them angrily through clenched teeth. Two more rounds shrieked past her while she sat in the saddle, shocked and confused. The only reason she was not hit, was because Barney would not stand still. His adrenaline was high; he was in flight mode and he wanted to run.

She turned Barney and kicked him hard. He leaped forward, pushing through the water and making a great white wake in his rage to reach the creek bank. He stepped into a deep spot and they sank down again with a big splash, but his powerful swim stokes had them through it in seconds, He again found footing, and launched them up and out of the hole, with a series of powerful leaps. He reached the shallow water, splashing and thumping across a small sand bar.

Barney climbed up the bank and out of the creek, then with great effort, leaped up to the narrow trail with two powerful jumps, nearly losing Anne, then trotted dangerously through the dark, treacherous tunnel that led towards the safety of the foothills.

Begin Again

Anne rode Barney through the pre-dawn morning. He was hot and foamy around the saddle, and panting hard. But she kept on him, not letting up, as he heroically galloped up dark dirt paths and trotted through precarious trails that were so dim Anne could not see the path, so she would hug Barney's neck in these dark places, keeping her head low and safe from the sticks and branches that she could not see.

She could hear the weapons going off in the heavens. She knew nothing about nuclear missiles, or how they were supposed to work, but she knew what she was hearing: the booming of massive shock waves, followed by a faint rumbling roar. The explosions became rapid and continuous, and as they grew louder, they became more rapid, as if the entire reserve of Earth's nuclear arsenal had been launched into the fight. She could only compare it to a long string of nuclear firecrackers going off, hundreds of detonations in quick succession. A very long and terrifying string of destruction, that lasted many long minutes. The atmosphere was beginning to flex from the pressure of this novel defense, and Anne and

Barney could feel it. The shock waves from space were compressing the skies and causing Anne to feel heavy. Her ears began to ring, and her head felt full. Barney let out an unusual whinny and shook his head. Anne knew he felt it too. She slowed him down and let him walk. She knew he had done more than she should have allowed.

They emerged from a brush line deer trace and into a clearing. She climbed down sorely from Barney and began to lead him across an open meadow. The dawn was arriving and the sky began to change from black to the darkest cobalt blue, a sign that the new day had arrived.

Last night was supposed to be 'the last night', she thought to herself. *But it wasn't. The asteroid must have missed. The nuclear weapons launched into space must have worked*. She stopped and suddenly turned around to look at Barney.

"You think it worked?" she asked the tired horse.

Barney, still panting, flared his nostrils and let out a weak snort.

Anne reached around Barney's big neck with both arms, and hugged him tightly and lovingly. She cried into his mane. She could smell the sweat and the blood, as she held her face tight to his neck and breathed in deep. Then quietly, she whispered to him, "Adela saved us. She saved the world."

She wasn't absolutely sure if was really true, but she knew, absolutely, that Adela's mission was intended to preserve the planet. And maybe her contribution was the little detail that made the difference. She would never know. But for now, to honor the sincerest effort of her friend, she would say it.

She loosened up on Barney and began to lead him through a field of tall, dry grass. The pre-sunrise landscape was now dominated by a mellow pink sky. She could see a distant storm approaching.

The first birds were out and looking for seeds. Their little silhouettes against the emerging pinkish sky were a hopeful sight for her, and she watched them. Occasionally, she would stop to marvel at how the individual birds of the flock seemed to read each other's mind; maneuvering together, as if in one collective thought. And what she thought looked like a monogamous couple; two birds wanting to stay with each other, and foraging together.

She soon realized that the dawn had left her out in the open with the first light. And that was a bad place to be. She turned to look about for signs of meat hunters. She would walk about thirty paces, stop, and turn around a full three hundred and sixty degrees, nervously scanning the horizon for any unusual sign.

She walked in front of Barney, leading him to the edge of the open field's brush line. She found a narrow trail that seemed to start at a low hanging juniper bough. She pushed the branch forward, and saw that the trail continued, so she continued. When she was through, she gently let the branch fall on Barney's chest, and he let it brush by him as he walked past it. When he was through, the bough snapped back into place with a whip like rush, and then they were gone, into the safety of the forest.

The End